The Melton-Uppbury Village Mystery's

The Twitchers Invasion and the Monks Return

Sebastian Blanchard

CONTENTS

Dr Clutterbuck Introduces Readers to The Village of Melton-Uppbury

Chapter

1 The Priory Bird Watchers Club

2 The Monk in the Rectory Garden

3 A Rare Bird Sighting

4 The Clutterbucks call in the Archaeologists

5 Rare Bird Sighting Confirmed

6 Archaeologists Dig Up the Rectory Garden

7 The Twitchers Invasion

8 The Riding school gets a new owner

9 The Village Remembers Remembers It's Fallen Heroes

10 Dorothy gets an Indecent Proposal

11 The Angry Tall Thin Man

12 The Monks get a Christian Burial

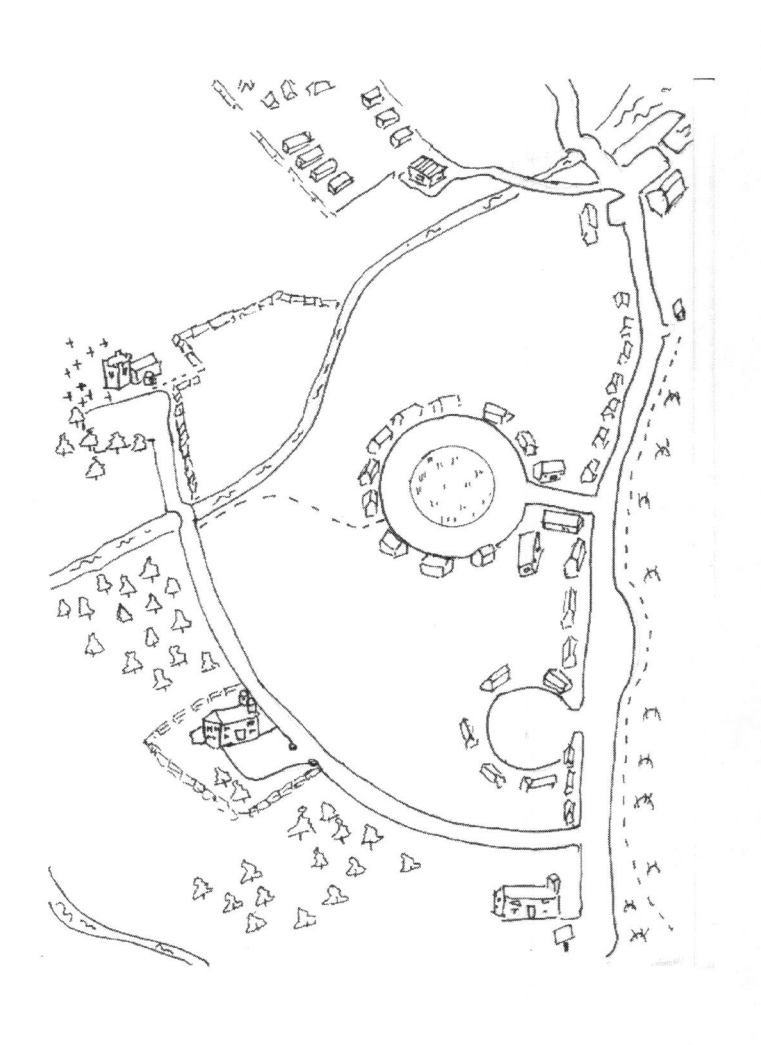

The Village of Melton-Uppbury

An Introduction to the Village of Melton-Uppbury

The Old Rectory
Church Lane
Melton-Uppbury
East Lincolnshire

Dear Reader,

I would like to tell you a little about the village I live in with my wife Julie, we live in the old Rectory close by the church of St Guthlac's.

The tranquil village of Melton-Uppbury is situated on the East Coast of Lincolnshire surrounded by fenland. It's a small close knit community with limited local amenities, and a population of around 150, which is increased during the summer season due to it having a small caravan park situated to the north of the village just past the boatyard on the west fenland side of the main road.

The village was formerly a hamlet called Melton and co-existed alongside the Priory of Uppbury, which was established around 1343 by a group of Augustinian monks. Last year we found out more about the history of our village thanks to research done by Mrs Barrhead our retired librarian. The priory of 1343 is built on the site of an earlier monastic house; which may have been destroyed by fire about the same time that the Celtic Priory of St Aidan on Lindisfarne (Holy Island) in Northumberland was sacked by the Vikings in 793. It is believed that some followers of St Guthlac of Crowland Abbey built the original wooden priory perhaps initially with just a few cells and a wooden chapel.

In 1535 Henry VIII dissolved the Uppbury Priory, but being just a small establishment and only owning a hundred or so acres of land it was not handed to any of his friends or supporter's, as was the fate of most monastic houses at that time, it was just abandoned. By the 1700s almost every residue of its former structural above ground level remains had been robbed out and used in the building of the popular nearby seaside resort of Reedsthorpe. One archway in the present Rectory may be connected with the said priory, although believed to be Norman it could be from another nearby former manor house demolished at about the time the Rectory was built in 1915.

The village took the name Melton-Uppbury in 1850 to commemorate its monastic origins. The village church is dedicated to St Guthlac; we have our own incumbent Vicar, the Rev Rosemary Fitter thanks to the benevolence of our local Inn landlord Col James Smith-Fitzroy the last descendant of the family, which owned the estate upon which the village was built.

It has a row of pretty cottages that stretch along the main road facing the dunes and sea, with a small bungalow complex built behind them, along with a small council house estate. Entering the village from the south, a lane to the left just past the Crows Roost Inn before you reach the sea front cottages, leads along church lane, to the back of the council estate passing my house the Old Rectory and on to the car park of St Guthlac's Church.

Local amenities consist of a post office cum general store, that serves as the villages gossip centre run by Harry and Kate Weatherspoon, this stands on Sea View Street next to the village Library at the entrance to the council estate, opposite is the Village Hall managed by the Parish Council. Sea View Street is second turn left on the main road north bound past Church Lane, cutting through the row of seafront cottages. The only other shop is the Pestell Emporium, an antiques shop owned by Silas Pestell and this is the very last building at the north end of the village, or the first on the right coming southwards. Set in the dunes is the Beachside Café owned by Patsy Clyde. One other small business is Fred Allsop's Boat Yard, which is opposite Pestell's Antiques Emporium, and has a small inlet where seafarers can moor up to collect gas and other bits and pieces of chandlery. There is a narrow river, which is tidal coming into the boatyard complex from the fens via the village. It is navigable for small-motorised boats, but not wide enough for sailing dinghies to tack along it.

Our Local The Crows Roost Inn

The local pub is the Crows Roost Inn; which is a few yards or so south of village set back from the road with a car park to the front of it; which faces the road and dunes. To its rear is a pub garden, very popular in the summer months with tourists, which overlooks the back of the old rectory and church and a very old raucous rookery, from whence it got its name. The Inn is a free house owned and run by Col James Smith-Fitzroy.

The local garden Centre is situated half way between the village and the seaside resort of Reedsthorpe to the south and it is owned by the Rufford family.

Generally speaking Melton-Uppbury is a rather typical English Seaside Village, very quiet indeed in the winter months, in fact some residents go for days without seeing anyone other than the postman or paper man. In the summer it's often a hive of activity even though its not really noted as a seaside resort.

The small caravan park is usually fully booked in the summer months, and the Weatherspoon's appreciate the extra custom they get in the shop, and Harry delivers the daily papers to the site office when the site is open. Mrs Slater, who lives in the north end cottage on the main road, owns the site. She and her late husband owned Home Farm that the site is on, and when she lost her husband fifteen years ago, she sold the farm and all the land except the Caravan site which she kept on as a hobby, and brought her little cottage. The farm was sold to Cyril Merrick, and the stables and two paddocks went to his cousin John Merrick. The caravan park is in the field next to the Pestell's Antique Emporium at the north end of the village.

I invite you to read how a normally peaceful hobby such as bird watching can cause so much havoc and mayhem in a small community, that you may never think about bird watchers in the same light again. Added to which we will disclose what really was buried in my once beautiful garden, the state of my garden at present could make any garden lover cry, as my wife Julie has often done recently.

Yours Sincerely,

Dr Nigel Clutterbuck

PS.

A short catch up from the village affairs of last year:

Ghosts of Monks and a Viking warrior were seen by various villagers, mainly in the sand dunes, usually amidst a cloud of weird mist over a twelve-month period.

The Spring Fete was opened by the TV personality Charlie Dimmock an old school friend of our vicar the Rev Rosemary Fitter.

A large hoard of monastic treasure was found in a tomb in the church crypt thanks to the efforts of Dorothy Burton a theology student.

An archaeological dig took place on the beach and in the dunes, and some bones of a Viking Warrior and parts of his sword and shield along with his helmet were recovered. We gave the found bones a proper Viking Cremation at sea, on a specially commissioned scaled down replica Viking Long boat.

My wife Julie accidently uncovered some ancient bones when she tried to extend one of our flowerbeds. They had to be reburied by myself because it caused my wife a lot of distress at the time.

Our local church St Guthlacs was to be closed down, but the treasure find, helped secure its future.

Chapter 1

The Priory Bird Watching Club

It was mid February in the tranquil village of Melton-Uppbury, the winter had past quietly with only an occasional flurry of snow. Bitter icy cold winds had prevailed as usual for this part of the coast, even in the hot summers the cool winds tended to stop people from getting too hot, as opposed to the west coast resorts receiving all the benefits of the gulf stream and few bitter cold winds. The villagers were as one might say stirring from their winter's hibernation, and getting out and about.

The local pub the Crows Roost Inn was beginning to get a little bit busier again. The Innkeeper Col James Smith-Fitzroy hated January and February, only his die-hard regulars kept the pub going. In reality it cost James more during those times to open up than if he'd closed up instead, but living in the flat above the Inn he appreciated the little bit of company he got during that quiet period, even if it was only Jake from the estate or Len the Church Sexton propping up the bar.

The local bird watching club the Priory Birders as they were known, were in the corner of the Crows Roost lounge planning their, Spring and Summer outings programme. They were an odd assortment of characters not all from the village. The youngest was Sophie Weatherspoon; sixteen-year-old daughter of the local shop owners who only joined the group on a whim last year because a young man called Geoffrey had joined the group when he and his parents moved to the village last year.

Old Bill Taylor who lived in the bungalows with his wife Shelia set up the group when he retired five years ago, his wife was roped in to act as group secretary. He has an old mini bus so is able to take most of the non-car owning club members on their various outings to nature reserves and occasionally other places of interest. One of their biggest events of the year was the annual trip to the RSPB headquarters the Lodge at Sandy in Bedfordshire, where they would get a guided tour behind the scenes, walk the bird watching walk and culminate the day with a meal at the RSPBs restaurant. Mrs Slater, who owned the village caravan site, was a member as was Mrs Bottomly, but her attendance depended upon her priority duties as Chair of the St Guthlac's Church Council. Sidney Harding an accountant, who lived in nearby Reedsthorpe had also joined recently, he was also an active member of the Melton-Uppbury Historical Group, which was formed last year. He really liked the village and the locals, he was keeping his eye out for a house to come up for sale, so he could move to the village and feel more a part of the village community. Felicity Oundle a single thirty something year old nurse from Reedsthorpe had also recently joined. Strangely Reedsthorpe the nearest local town although being quite a large town had no bird or wildlife clubs.

At the north end of the village Silas Pestell of Pestells Antiques Emporium, a small antiques shop really, was busy cleaning up his shop in preparation he hoped for an early tide of visitors looking for that extra special something as Spring approached. Fred Allsop the boatyard owner across the road came over to see what he was up to, having got fed up with waiting for work to come in, and you can only do so much tidying up after all. 'Hello Silas, are you expecting visitors?'

Looking up Silas replied, 'Don't be so bloody cheeky, don't see any punters queuing up with orders in your yard neither.' 'Your right there, Silas, but last year was good though, but mainly repairs and sales of chandlery only new boat order was that Viking Funeral one and that went up in flames,' he chuckled as Silas laughed out aloud and yelled out, 'Come on Fred upstairs lets have a dram or two, I'm fed up with trying to make the place look anything more than a charity bric a brac shop.' He put up the closed sign on the door and led the way up to the flat.

Enid Barrhead the villages retired librarian, had taken her dog Truffles for his last walk of the day along the Beach, and met up with Gerald Parker who owned the busy general store in Reedsthorpe and lived in the village. He was bringing his pair of Red Setters onto the beach, and as the beach was clear of people and dogs, he let them off their leads to run down to the sea. 'No more strange happenings about here I hope Enid?' he asked referring to events that taken the village by storm last year; but were now gradually fading in every ones memory. 'No thank goodness, but I'm not convinced we have quite cleared the matter up yet,' she exclaimed. 'You might be right there Enid but lets hope its over at least for now.' They bid each other goodnight and went their separate ways.

Kate and Harry Weatherspoon were preparing to close up their post office cum local store. Harry called out, 'Where's Sophie, Kate?' continuing, 'I haven't seen her since she came in from school, in her room again on that machine I bet.' Kate shouted out, 'She won't be long she's at the Pub, its that bird club night.' 'Hope she's not drinking,' Harry piped up. 'You know James will make sure she only gets pop and crisps, he never lets anyone have a drink underage you know that,' proclaimed Kate.

The Priory Birders were finishing their last drinks and getting their coats on. The meeting had gone well, a timetable of trips had been sorted out and a little to the consternation of Bill Taylor, the group had agreed not to visit the RSPB Lodge this year, but had opted spend a day at the Bird Fair at Rutland Water in August instead. As they bid their farewells to the landlord thanking him for his hospitality, Sophie hung about the doorway hoping Geoffrey would offer to walk her home. Geoffrey however was too busy trying to find out more about the bird Fair from Felicity Oundle, who had suggested it as a great place to visit, she it appears was the only one who had ever been there, apparently with an x boyfriend a few years ago. So the pair of them stood in the car park talking. Felicity had to drive home to her parents house in Reedsthorpe, she was still saving up to buy her own place, having decided after her last relationship breakup she would be better living on her own. Geoffrey realised that Felicity was quite keen on bird watching, and knew quite a bit more about it than he did, he also knew that Sophie was definitely not so keen since she had so many other interests. So he was thinking that he might just, in time be able to spend days out with Felicity, the trouble was he was also keen on Sophie, and she was clearly attracted to him for reasons no one could explain. Geoffrey was a nice enough chap but no oil painting, in fact he was perhaps a bit of a geek, lanky with an unkempt look about him, not that his mother did not try to keep the twenty year old tidied up as best she could.

Sophie was still fidgeting around the doorway, having turned down a number of offers to walk her home by some of the locals, she soon realised that Geoffrey was a little more than taken with Felicity, but she thought he was being daft because he was much younger than her. In the end Sophie gave up and stormed past the pair and headed home in a temper.

Harry Weatherspoon was just about to lock the shop door when Sophie brushed past him very red and flushed in the face and raced directly upstairs to her bedroom slamming the door in the process. 'Oh dear,' said Kate to Harry when he came up to the flat, 'Seems the Bird Club Meeting didn't go too well.' 'I bet it's got something to do with that young Geoffrey Thompson,' said Harry scratching his head in wonderment and dismay at the temper tantrums his daughter had been displaying just lately. Kate said, 'Don't worry Harry she'll soon come out of it, don't forget she's off to the Lincoln Museum on Saturday to meet up with Zoe Lake that Archaeologist who did that dig here last year. She's promised to show our Sophie behind the scenes some of the work archaeologists do when not in the public gaze, and I think she said that Dorothy the Vicars last year student is meeting them for lunch, you know the one who found the treasure.' 'Of course I remember her, they will be good company for our Sophie I'm sure.' 'I thought you might,' said Kate winking at Harry.

Bird Fair Visit Organised

Sheila Taylor was busy at her study desk, typing up the minutes of yesterdays Bird club Meeting, when her husband Bill popped his head through the door. 'See your getting the club bits and pieces written up!' he exclaimed. 'Someone has to do it, you wont will you,' protested Shelia. Ignoring her moans he said, 'Tell you what, while your computers on how about finding out a bit about that Bird Fair, can't be as good as our normal outing I'm sure, but we'll have to book tickets I suppose.' Shelia quickly put her task aside and started googling for Bird Fairs. Soon the screen was filled with a large Bird Fair Notice:

Rutland Water Bird Fair August 10TH 11TH AND 12TH

3 Days of Glorious Birding Events for just £10 per person per day, children free

Special Optical Sales Telescopes and Binoculars, Digital scoping Aids

Meet the Experts get the best out of your bird watching

Spring Watch Personalities in attendance: Bill Oddie, Kate Humble, and Chris Packham

Bars, Restaurants, Play Areas, Bird Watching Centre

'Actually it sounds like a good day out,' said Shelia, 'And don't forget you always said you wanted to visit Rutland Water to see the Ospreys breeding.' Bill muttered in response to Shelia's enthusiasm, 'It'll be too late for the Ospreys they'll be long fled the nest.' Shelia said, 'Trust you to be negative, why don't we visit Rutland for a preview, if we time it right you'll see them then.' That thought cheered Bill up enormously, 'Okay then we'll do just that.'

Chapter 2

The Monk in the Rectory Garden

One evening in early March, Nigel and Julie Clutterbuck who lived in the Old Rectory were just getting ready to retire for the night at the Rectory. They had spent the evening at the Reedsthorpe Play House watching a pre-view of an amateur production of, '*A Mid Summer Nights Dream*,' that was due to open to the public later in the year. Julie had helped out at the theatre behind the scenes for a year or so now, but really was hoping to make her debut on stage sometime. The Playhouse Director self-appointed: had picked up early on Julies organisational skills and done his uttermost to keep her off the stage to act as his unpaid and unappreciated PA. He was a hopeless organiser, he just liked ordering people about and taking the credit for all that went well, but when things went wrong as they often did in this field of entertainment, it could all be blamed on Julie or the actors or anyone in fact, that he chanced to come across when these misfortunes occurred.

As Julie was closing the bedroom curtains, she looked out at the garden and tried to imagine that summer was upon them and that her flower borders were in full bloom. She was quickly brought down to earth when she saw a movement near the end of one of her flower borders, the one she had wanted to extend last summer, a job that had to be put off because she had uncovered a number of bones apparently human, which had so upset her. She remembered, when Nigel had to take her back into the house, and rebury the bones. Something she had tried hard to forget, but it was ever lingering in the back of her thoughts.

A cowled figure was standing exactly where she had been working that summer's day; she couldn't discern any features, in fact being quite dark it was all a bit obscure. Strangely she wasn't frightened just a bit taken aback. 'Nigel quick look out here I think its one of those monks again,' she called out. Last year there had been a number of sightings of what people perceived to be ghostly monks, even the vicar had seen one in the church. Nigel got to the window as fast as he could but by the time his eyes had adjusted to the outside darkness the figure had vanished. He said, 'Come on dear, its been a busy evening try and get settled, you've not opened the covers of that library book you got out last week yet have you, the one about that chap and his wife who sold their house and bought a houseboat down in the midlands.'

Back at the shop Sophie had settled down a bit after her upset with Geoffrey, when her mother reminded her of her invitation to Lincoln next Saturday, to see the museums archaeological collections; after all Sophie had claimed last year that her real goal in life was to be an archaeologist like Zoe the Lincoln Museum Archaeologist or was it Lara Croft. Zoe now Mrs Hartington who got married in Melton-Uppbury last year could help Sophie prepare for entry to a University that taught Archaeology, so it was as well that she had taken up Zoe's invitation to go to the museum.

Sophie had taken up an interest in Archaeology as soon as she started at Reedsthorpe Comprehensive School a few years ago, where one of the teachers was a qualified archaeologist, and last year when a museum team had excavated the nearby beach and sand dunes, and found some Viking bones, and other associated relics, such as a Viking helmet she had the opportunity to work as a volunteer digger on the site, between doing her school and college work. She had also joined the local historical group, set up by Dr Nigel Clutterbuck, and Gerald Parker the chairman of the local Parish Council. Nigel was a keen amateur archaeologist, and had a study full of books and documents about archaeology and history, these he allowed Sophie to use whenever she had time, and he too like Zoe, very much supported young Sophie's archaeological ambitions. Nigel and his wife Shelia enjoyed having the occasional visits made to their house by young Sophie, she had such a spirited and ever adventuresome personality, and she enlivened their normally quite mundane lives. Many a time Sophie's parents Harry and Kate had come out looking for her, and found her engrossed in books in Nigel's study, or splayed out on the Clutterbuck's conservatory floor surrounded by Nigel's collection of archaeological artefacts.

Dorothy at College

Dorothy Burton was busy studying in her little bedsit in Lincoln for her next exam at the Lincoln Theological College, and trying to work out if she could afford to take time out from study to meet

Zoe and Sophie for lunch on Saturday. Her mind was made up when she received a call from her friend Rosemary Fitter Rector of St Guthlac's Church in Melton-Uppbury, where she spent three exciting months last year.

'Might not have lunch with Zoe and Sophie, not got time, too much study to do!' Dorothy told Rosemary. 'Stuff, and Nonsense,' shouted Rosemary through the telephones earpiece. 'But, But,' Dorothy tried to explain but was defeated when Rosemary yelled, 'We women have to stick together, it's a Woman's world now, the men had, had their chance and blew it, it's our turn now.' Dorothy knew that Rosemary was all bluster and certainly not anti-men but the carry on at the time of the first women's ordinations in England had certainly had an affect on her. In fact Rosemary had confided in her that she wasn't at all sure why she wanted to be a vicar and felt pushed into it at times by the huge feminist lobby in the Church of England. Rosemary had accepted that many a good male candidate had been turned down to make way for the feminist cause.

However her reasoning was that lots of occupations had been for time immemorial male only, and generally archaeology was one of them, so they had a duty to encourage young Sophie to follow in Zoe's footsteps.

Apart from which Dorothy really liked Zoe and they had become quite good friends, and in Sophie she saw a younger version of herself. So she decided to abandon her studies to meet them as she had initially agreed to anyway.

The Monks Second Appearance

Harry and Silas along with Alf Prichard were slowing walking home by the cottages on the main road having indulged in a few pints at the Crows Roost, when Alf noticed a mist rising in the dunes exactly as it had done on may occasions last year just by the cut through to the beach. Harry and Silas ignored Alf's assertions that he could see a figure in the mist, through the darkness of the evening. 'But look' look, It's a bloody monk, I swear it is!' he cried out in vain as the other two walked on and headed straight up to Silas's shop flat for yet another nightcap. Alf forlornly turned into Sea View Street and headed to his home on the estate.

Pestells Antiques Emporium

Up at the antiques shop flat, Silas who was in his late sixties poured Fred a generous malt whiskey. 'Don't you think we have had a bit too much already,' said Fred at the same time supping a great slurp of the golden nectar as they both called it.
'I don't think so; after all didn't you hear Alf saying he had seen another ghost. Lets drink a toast to the monks of Uppbury Priory.'

Lunchtime at the Crows Roost for Julie and Enid

Enid Barrhead met up with Julie Clutterbuck; for lunch as they occasionally did at the Crows Roost Inn, it was early April. 'Well ladies what can we serve you today?' asked Col James. 'Is it something off the light bite menu or the regular one?' Julie replied, 'I think I'd rather have a drink first that will give us time to peruse your menu, if you don't mind James.' Enid nodded in agreement, not really feeling very hungry, but not wanting to miss out on a few pleasant hours to talk to Julie. Since she had lost her husband and retired she had found life quite lonely if it wasn't for her daily visit to Weatherspoons shop for her paper she might not speak to anyone apart from the occasional other dog walkers on some days. 'Right ladies give me a shout when your ready I'll just get your drinks, usual is it? 'Thanks,' responded Enid.

'Well Julie have you heard about Alf Pritchard seeing another monk in the dunes up by my house a few nights ago?' 'No,' she said, as a cold shiver ran down her spine. Enid related to her how she had heard Alf telling Harry in the shop all about it, and how Silas and Fred thought it was Alf's wishful thinking, since he hoped there was still more treasure to be found. Julie decided to confide in Enid what she herself had seen from her bedroom window a few weeks ago.

Enid tried to take in what Julie had told her and exclaimed, 'I knew it wasn't over, I said so as much to Mr Parker some time ago.' She went on to outline what she thought might be going on as they started the first course of the lunch. 'You see Julie, last year as you will remember we saw the Viking remains sent out to sea and back to Valhalla, so whilst we settled his situation, as his appearances had basically seemed to ask us too, we didn't and couldn't address the monks cries for help, as I see it anyway.'

'Yes I see where your coming from, so if we could find the remains of the monks and give them a Christian burial it might end the appearances!' 'Yes,' replied Enid, 'I think that's what I'm trying to say, I suppose.' 'Enid you know when you did that research last year about the Religious Communities along the east coast, didn't you say something about the monks leaving Lindisfarne with the relics of St Cuthbert.' 'Yes they had to leave in a hurry with their families, treasures and the bones of St Cuthbert.' Julie cried out did you say they had their families with them?' 'Yes, of course they couldn't leave them the Vikings were expected and they weren't known for their pity or mercy, they would have killed the children and killed or taken the women for themselves,' explained Enid. 'So any bones that might be found here of any monks, might also have children's bones with them,' asked Julie. 'Oh yes the Vikings would have killed them as well undoubtedly.'

Julie then asked Enid how it was that the monks had families surely monks were celibate, how come they had children. 'Well from what I have been able to find out, the early monastic's in Britain did not have a vow of chastity. In fact the Monastery Abbot in those times was often married, and when he died or retired the Abbacy was taken over by his son or the next in the family line.' 'Heavens I really did not know that, so the cries of children you heard in the dunes last year could have been the monks own children being slaughtered?' said Julie quite surprised. Enid went on, 'I now fear so, you know the leader of the Lindisfarne community who led the community to safety with the relics of St Cuthbert was Bishop Aldhun and he had a family, in fact his daughter was married to the then Earl of Northumbria Uchtred.'

Julie was quite perturbed by the thought that not only monks but also women and children were probably cut to pieces or endured even a more appalling a fate, right here close to their own homes. Julie had found bones, including a child's skull in her garden last summer, she had got in such a state that her husband Dr Clutterbuck had ushered her back into the house, and reburied the bones. He had come to the conclusion that since they lived in a rectory built on the site of a former monastery such finds were inevitable and nothing to be concerned about. Julie Clutterbuck had wanted to tell Enid about the bones, but thought she had better talk to her husband first. The thought of police and archaeologists digging up her beloved garden was dreadful.

So Julie resolved to talk to Nigel about the bones, despite her upset at the very thought of people being buried in her garden she couldn't let her personal wishes perhaps hide the truth forever, and stop these poor long lost souls from being given a proper pathway to heaven.

Sophie makes her Career Choice

'How did your day go then?' asked Kate Weatherspoon, as her daughter Sophie came into the shop having just got off the Melton-Louth-Lincoln bus across the road. 'It was great mum, Zoe's fantastic she told me so much I can't take it all in, and the things they have stored away in the museum is unbelievable. There's a huge leg bone of an elephant a femur I think she said, found not far from here in the 1800s.'

'Sounds great, did you go for a meal?' asked her mother. Sophie went on to say, how they spent till two o clock in the museum, because her bus didn't get to Lincoln till half ten. So Zoe rang Dorothy and changed the time they were going to meet. 'So we ended up in a Yates pub, as Dorothy said cheap but good food.' 'We all went back to the museum for a bit then Dorothy said she'd drive me to Louth because the next through bus from Lincoln would not be till six thirty, so they both thought it better that I did not get home too late, and the bus service to Melton from Louth is quite regular.

Dorothy waited at the bus station with me till the bus came.' 'How nice of her,' Kate said. 'Better still mum, Zoe said if I went over again I could stay over with her and her husband Mick, you know the other archaeologist who did our Beach Dig last year, if you and dad are okay with it.' 'That fine, I suppose it will stop you moping about Geoffrey, if your keener on archaeology than bird watching that is.' 'That's what you think', Sophie muttered under her breath as she headed for her room with her bag full of leaflets and archaeology course information that Zoe had collected for her. 'And by the way mum I'm definitely going to train to be an archaeologist just like Lara Croft!' Shutting her bedroom door firmly as soon as she'd said it. Harry and Kate had hoped she'd just want to help in the shop and eventually take it over, but she had shown no inclination to do so. In fact she hated the shop, living in the flat above the shop there was no peace to study. Her mum and dad got up early for the papers and worked till ten most evenings, it being the only shop in the village. Mum and dad were far too busy to pay her much attention or so she wrongly thought. Fortunately Sophie was of a nature that she was self reliant, and easily made friends along with a great curiosity about life so was by way of an active teenager, always seeking new things to do and projects to complete. Much liked by all who happened to meet her. It was that nature and temperament that so attracted Rosemary and Dorothy to her.

The Bitterns and the Angry Man

A few days later Geoffrey called in at the Weatherspoons shop, 'Hello Mrs Weatherspoon I was wondering if Sophie was in, I'm going down to Sprig Point Nature Reserve, there's some Bitterns there I want to see, wondering if Sophie would like to come with me?' 'You'd better ask her yourself she's in her room upstairs third room on the left, be sure to knock first,' said Kate. 'Thanks Mrs Weatherspoon,' he yelled as he bounded up the stairs. Sophie heard him bounding up the stairs like a gazelle, no one else made such a commotion. She opened her bedroom door and shouted, 'What, the hell do you want Geoffrey Thompson.' 'To see if you want to visit Sprig Point Nature Reserve, I'm off there now and thought you might be a bit bored so called on the off chance,' he explained. 'Wasn't your Old friend Felicity Oundle free, or has she realised she's almost old enough to be your mother,' Sophie cried out. Overhearing her daughter's anger, Kate yelled up the stairs, 'Get yourself out Sophie you could do with some fresh air.' After a little persuasion, and Geoffrey promising he was only interested in Felicity as a bird watching club member, as he himself had realised she was far out of his reach anyway. Sophie agreed to go. She quickly set about making up a small packed lunch and getting changed into her outdoor gear.

As they sat on the top deck of the bus as it drove down the main road towards Reedsthorpe, Geoffrey tried his hardest to interest Sophie in the passage of seabirds they could see out of the window flying over the sea southwards. All of a sudden Sophie grabbed Geoffrey's arm pointing over to the windows overlooking the inland fenlands and cried out, 'Look, what's that, is it an Eagle?' Geoffrey looked to where Sophie was pointing and saw a huge eagle type bird flying high in a circular movement. 'No it's not, it's a Common Buzzard,' he said. 'But its huge I can see its very high up there, but it must have a wing span of over six feet,' protested Sophie, 'Surely only eagles are that big?' Geoffrey got out his Collins Bird Guide and showed Sophie pages 76 and 90:

Golden Eagle Length 80-93cm. Wing Span 190-225cm.

Common Buzzard Length 46-58cm. Wing Span 110-132cm.

'So Sophie you see, the buzzard is a big bird but quite a bit smaller than the eagle, but it's by far the biggest Raptor we see in this region.' 'What's a Raptor?' asked Sophie.

'It's a term that means simply a bird of prey,' he explained. They went on to discuss the differences of size and colour, between the eagles and buzzard families. They were still engrossed in an in-depth discussion about the way one could distinguish between the *Accipitridae*: The Hawks, Buzzards and Eagles and the *Falconidae:* Falcons, like their recent Icelandic gyrfalcon sighting, peregrines and kestrels, when the bus pulled into a lay by near the dunes. A large brown notice board read:

SPRIG POINT NATURE RESERVE

Please keep to the footpaths. Dogs must be

kept on leads at all times, use dog-waste bins provided.

Wardens Patrol this Reserve

In Emergency Telephone Reedsthorpe 6888998

Geoffrey checked with the driver the times for buses going back, to Reedsthorpe and on to Melton-Uppbury. They adjusted their rucksacks, and Geoffrey led the way crossing the road towards the Fenland Walkway, after about half an hour Sophie yelled, 'Geoffrey how much further are we going, I need a sit down and drink.' 'Okay the first Hides just down here we'll rest up there if you like.' He led her down a small sidetrack, they climbed a small set of steps, as they opened the door, the expected waft of mustiness and wood hit them. Geoffrey opened all the viewing flaps and a cool fresh light wind came through them blowing much of the mustiness out through the door they had left open.

Sprig Point Bird Watching Hide

They looked out to see a huge reed bed, with occasional small pockets of open water, which were populated by dozens of coots. As Geoffrey looked down towards the ground at the front of the hide, near the waters edge in the reeds he saw a movement, he beckoned Sophie over, 'Look,' he pointed down to a brown bird going in and out of the reed bed. 'What is it?' whispered Sophie. 'It's a Water Rail,' he quietly replied. They settled down sitting on the narrow benches of the Hide, and poured out their drinks. Sophie handed Geoffrey a mars bar, and chomped away at her own. She had nicked them from the shop, her parents Kate and Harry, had always known who the culprit was that kept emptying the chocolate bar shelf. Harry said of the missing mars bars, 'At least we don't have to worry about Sophie going anorexic like some of her college friends do we.' So they happily turned a blind eye to Sophie's chocolate addiction. After all she was quite slim to average in build, so the chocolate was in no way leading her to becoming obese, as the media kept suggesting a lot of young people were now.

Geoffrey said, 'I think we had better get a move on to the next hide if we want to see the bitterns, before its time to get back for the bus. They quickly packed their bits and pieces, as Geoffrey looked over to Sophie and very quietly said, 'Do you think we might go out properly some time?' 'What do you mean, like proper boy and girl friend?' she said hesitantly. 'Well I suppose so, I know I'm a little bit older than you, and, well not as good looking as some, but I really like you,' he blushed as the words left his mouth. Sophie said, 'I'll think about it, but if you knock about with that felicity woman again you can get stuffed,' she blurted out.

They walked on another half a mile or so, when Geoffrey turned round to Sophie and said, 'We are nearly there now, we will have to be very quiet,' as he said this they heard a loudish, 'Boom' 'Boom' echo across the reed beds ahead of them. 'What's that?' exclaimed Sophie loudly. 'Its them, it's them!' he said putting his finger to his lips making it clear to Sophie they had to be quiet. They crept up to the hide, and as quiet as mice went in, but Sophie's rucksack caught the door handle and made it clatter, a man with his back to them was taking continuous photos of something in the reed beds, he turned round angrily glaring at Sophie, 'How dare you interrupt me,' said the tall thin man wearing a combat jacket, he was pale and had a twisted moustache. Geoffrey stepped between them and said, leave my girl friend alone, it was an accident. The man backed off, faced with a tall gawky young man holding his fist out and his girl friend getting ready to have a go as well. 'Sorry,' he blurted out and turned back to his photography.

Geoffrey and Sophie went and sat on the benches at the far end of the hide, and got their binoculars out. Geoffrey got out his Collins Bird guide, and pointed to the images of Bitterns. Sophie looked intently at the pictures, and turned back to carefully surveying the reeds, looking for a brown bird that looked like a reed.

It wasn't long before Geoffrey realised that the angry man was actually photographing a pair bitterns, just a few metres from the hide. He got up without saying anything and stood behind Sophie, as she looked back he put his finger to his mouth again. He then gently grabbed her shoulders and carefully directed her towards the bitterns, adjusting the focus ring on her binoculars she saw clearly the image of a bittern it was just like the pictures in the bird book, it had its beak pointing to the sky and was really well camouflaged into the reed bed landscape. They had been there quite a while when Geoffrey looked at his watch and realised, it was time to head back to the bus stop.

The Reed bed where they saw the Bitterns

As they walked back along the track passing the first Hide they had stopped at, they ate their sandwiches, in the excitement of seeing the bitterns, and having to tread on eggshells in the second Hide because of the angry man they had forgotten to have their lunch, in the second Hide as they had planned. Back at the bus stop, having another ten minutes to wait they sat on the verge and finished their flasks of coffee and juices. 'It's been a nice day out Geoffrey, thank you for asking me,' said Sophie. Geoffrey blushed saying, 'Glad it wasn't too boring for you Sophie, I know you'd rather be digging up ancient bones and things.'

Back in Melton-Uppbury, Geoffrey left Sophie at the door of her shop, giving her a tiny peck on the cheek as he headed off to his parents house on the green, with a happy grin on his face.

Kate Weatherspoon eyed her daughter coming in and heading for the stairs to the flat and yelled over to her 'Good day Sophie?' 'Just ordinary,' she replied, but she had a smile on her face as she ascended the stairs.

Chapter 3

A Rare Bird Sighting

A week later twenty year old, Geoffrey Thompson headed off on his pushbike up to the Melton Washes Coastal Nature Reserve, which was just north of the village, he had hoped Sophie would come with him, but her dad said she was at college. He had packed his lunch, a flask of coffee and a couple of mars bars, for some reason mars bars made him think about Sophie. It wasn't a very warm day so he made sure he had a woolly jumper packed in his rucksack, he couldn't wear it riding his bike he would be too hot. With his binoculars slung around his neck and two bird reference books stuffed in his pockets he cycled past Fred Allsop's boatyard at speed heading north past Home Farm on his left. 'My what a sight,' thought Silas Pestell, as he watched young Geoffrey whizzing past his shop window a few minutes previously, thinking 'I wish I had that amount of youthful energy.'

As he neared his destination, glancing out to sea as he cycled, he thought he saw a peregrine falcon, scooting along the surface of the water. He put his brakes on and skidded to a halt in a gravel lay by overlooking the beach and sea. He propped his bike up against a section of fence, and put his binoculars to his eyes scanning the surface of the water. He could see nothing; a little disappointed he soon remounted his bike and continued his journey.

At the reserve he dismounted at the empty car park, and lifted his bike over the style, no mean feat when your loaded up with a rucksack, binoculars, books and spare clothing etc, he then walked along the little track towards the bird Hide which overlooked the sea to the east on one side and the fens and irrigation ditches on the other. He climbed the few steps up to the door of the hide, after leaning his bike at the side of a bank a few yards a way. He pushed the door wide open; the musty woody smell hit him directly. He quickly opened all of the Hides observation portals and propped them open, the light and cool breeze from the sea entered and very soon the hide smelt a little better.

The Hide Portals Geoffrey opened

Clearly no one had been in this particular Hide for ages. He got his books out and laid them out on a part of the wooden bench seating, carefully setting his binoculars on the ledge at one of the sea view portals, he then quickly set about pouring himself a coffee. Whilst drinking his steaming cuppa, he skimmed through his Collins Bird Guide, to page 98:

Peregrine Falcon

The peregrine falcon breeds on coastal cliffs or in mountains, also on cliffs in lowlands and on open bogs in taiga.

'Well there's no cliffs round here, only up at Bempton Rocks in East Yorkshire, but as the crow flies not too far I suppose,' he thought to himself, still convinced that it was a peregrine he had seen not so long ago. The book showed a picture of a peregrine flying with its whitish barred underbelly showing; he was sure that was what he had seen, but he had only got a momentary glance of it, he was sure none of the other falcons he had ever seen had quite such a distinctive light coloured under belly. So he set himself up to spend the rest of the day watching out for its return, he wished he had two heads so he could watch out to sea and across the fens at the same time. Whilst trying to be sure not to miss a sighting of the peregrine he managed to notch up a few of the commoner birds to his days tick list:

Open Sea and beach Viewings

2xCormorant
1xShag
20+Oystercatchers
50+Dunlin
20xRedshank
1xAvocet
1xHerring Gull
100+Black-baced Gulls
1xCommon Tern

Fenland and Lagoon Viewings

1X Curlew
1x Grey Heron
2x Great Crested Grebe
1x Little Owl
4x Little Grebe
1x Kestrel
5x Mallard
2X Coot

Just as darkness was falling, Geoffrey had all but given up on his quest to see the peregrine, his eyes were getting blurry, when he heard a low sort of chattering, it sounded like a peregrine he had heard on a tape sometime but it wasn't very distinct. Then he saw in the twilight a bird flying by at a terrific speed, it had long pointed wings and a tapered tail, and was a blur of white, which stood out in the enveloping darkness. It was on the fenland side of the Hide; he didn't have time to get his binoculars up to see what would have been a spectacular sight, but he was convinced now it was a peregrine. He sped off home on his cycle well excited, as all bird watchers are when they believe they have seen something special, but just how special he wouldn't find out for few days as yet.

Back home Geoffrey decided to pop round to see Bill Taylor and ask him what he thought about his sighting. Shelia opened the door of their bungalow; it was dark and far too late for callers she had thought when the doorbell rang out. 'Sorry it's so late but I wondered if I might have a few words with Bill,' he blurted out. 'Of course Geoffrey, go on through he's in the study.

Bill looked up from his desk in his tiny study, 'Geoffrey well what brings you round this time of night? Sit on this stool, sorry not much room in here for comfortable chairs,' welcomed Bill in his normally cheery way. Geoffrey couldn't help coughing a little as the smoke from Bills pipe crept into his lungs. 'Sorry Geoffrey but this is the only inside place I can smoke my pipe you know, don't get many visitors in here, perhaps that's why, ha, ha.'

Geoffrey's looked around Bills room, it was wall to wall bookshelves, overflowing with books, brochures and files of papers, most seemed to be about birds or wildlife. There was a case of stuffed birds on top of one of the bookcases; Geoffrey stood up to inspect its contents, a curlew and redshank and green sandpiper not that Geoffrey would have recognised the last one had it not been labelled. 'Ah so you found my little bird collection!' exclaimed Bill. 'I thought you weren't allowed to keep stuffed birds now,' Geoffrey said. 'Well normally that's quite right its been illegal to kill certain birds, in fact most birds since the 1950s, and in the 60s more legislation came in and egg collecting was banned. I certainly collected bird's eggs when I was a boy; most boys did in those days. But these birds were shot and stuffed by my grandfather in the late 1890s, so I am allowed to keep them, had to re-case them a couple of times over the years though.' 'Did you recognise the green sandpiper?' Geoffrey replied, 'No! I know the curlew there's lots about around here, and the redshank saw some last week but I've never seen a green sandpiper, to be honest I find the waders the most difficult to recognise.' 'Your not alone there young Geoff, I've spent a lifetime bird watching and never seem to get a close enough view of them to make an instant identification, anyway you haven't told me why you've come round.' Geoffrey went on to tell Bill about his two sightings of the peregrine.

Bill puffed away at his pipe for a while and said, 'Why do you think it's so special to see a peregrine Geoffrey?' 'It says in my book they only breed in certain places usually on cliffs and there's none round here are there, and I know I haven't been looking at birds for long, but I haven't seen one before, I don't think,' replied Geoffrey. Bill smiled and put his pipe in the ashtray, and got out a file of photos and handed it to Geoffrey.

He opened it and found lots of photos of peregrines nesting on church towers, even on old second-world war aerodrome control towers. 'So peregrine falcons don't need cliffs, my book says they do?' Bill explained how peregrines were not uncommon, and were breeding almost everywhere, there was a pair breeding on Lincoln Cathedral. 'They have been breeding there for about five years now,' Bill told him, he then quizzed Geoffrey.

'But didn't you say it seemed to be a very light or whitish bird?' 'Yes I think so, and it seemed quite big really, its wings seemed to be much bigger than a kestrel and I've seen lots of them, and definitely falcon shaped,' Geoffrey explained. Bill said, 'Well it sounds like a peregrine, but I have to say I haven't seen one along this part of the coast but I'm sure they must pass by occasionally, but no matter what a good sighting, a good sighting indeed.' Bill and Shelia saw Geoffrey out, Bill was thinking deeply. Shelia said, 'What's the matter Bill you look a little up tight?' 'Ah! It's nothing really but the way Geoffrey described the peregrine has made me think of another alternative, I'm sure I read about some sightings quite recently of a rare falcon not too far away. I'll have a look through some of my notes in the morning.'

Bill Identifies Geoffrey's Rare Bird

In the early hours after Geoffrey's evening visit; Bill was scuffling about in his study. 'What on earth are you doing in there at six in the morning, for heavens sake?' called out Shelia from the bedroom, having been disturbed by the noise Bill was making. He shouted through to her, 'Sorry love but that bird Geoffrey saw has been playing on my mind, but I think I may have it worked out, you see he made it very clear that what he saw was a peregrine shaped bird, but it was very light coloured in fact almost white, also it was not spiralling out of the sky after its prey as a peregrine would, it was seemingly chasing it along just above ground level.' By this time Shelia was out of bed and in her dressing gown hovering at Bills study door. 'What difference does that make?' she asked. Bill went on to hand her a sheet of paper he had just retrieved from his computer, 'I knew I had seen something that might just answer my questions,' Bill said to her. 'But Bill this is a list of reported sightings of a Gyrfalcon, what's that got to do with Geoffrey's peregrine.' Bill then explained to Shelia that she had in her hand a list of recent sightings of the rare Gyrfalcon not just anywhere but here in Lincolnshire. 'Look, three sightings off Read's Island on the Humber, and one down by Gibraltar Point, and that's in the last two weeks or so.' He took down some bird books off his study book shelves and located the pages referring to the Gyrfalcon, whilst he was doing this Shelia googled in Gyrfalcon on the computer:

Gyrfalcon from Wikipedia
The Gyrfalcon-Falco rusticolus-is the largest of the falcon species. It breeds on Arctic coasts and the islands of North America, Europe, and Asia. It is mainly a resident there also, but some Gyrfalcons disperse more widely after the breeding season, or in winter. Individual vagrancy can take birds for long distances.

'Well that's quite exciting but how can you prove it, Geoffrey's descriptions a bit vague and no one will accept his word for it will they?' put in Shelia. Bill said, 'We have to get a first hand sighting of it ourselves, and a photo that's the difficult job, the Read's Island sightings were only accepted when a lady got a photograph of one.' 'This is going to have to be a whole group exercise, we are going to need to cover our whole village coastline, and the fens at the back of the village, all hands on deck I'm afraid.' Bill immediately called a meeting of the Priory Birders at the Crows Roost Inn to outline his plans. He called young Geoffrey round to his bungalow to tell him that he thought his previous days sightings could be much more important than they had previously thought, and he told him of his plan to deploy their group members around the village setting up discreet observation stations.

The Birders Plan of Action

At the Crows Roost Inn the group gathered at 8 pm as directed, all were quite excited wondering what was going on. Bill had never called an emergency meeting like this before, and his phone calls had been very mysterious. Bill had decided that it was best at this early stage not to disclose too much, after all a Gyrfalcon being seen on his patch would be quite something.

Having explained to his small group the plan to try and get a confirmed sighting of a gyrfalcon he asked them who could spare possibly the whole of the next weekend. Strict instructions were given that this operation must be kept secret for the time being, to all intents and purposes this was to be a normal days local bird watching. All the members agreed to put some time in, but it was clear that only Geoffrey and Bill himself could spend a whole two days on the project. 'Well we will have to do a rota for each watching station,' said Shelia Taylor, 'But even then there aren't enough of us to do it because Bill has identified eight spotting points and we only have eight members so what are we to do?' Felicity interjected, 'I might be able to help, I'll see if I can recruit a few volunteers from the hospital, leave it with me for the time being.' Thanks Felicity, that would be a great help,' Bill said.

Clearly eight individual volunteers could not be expected to sit in tents or hides for two whole days without company or the opportunity to pop home occasionally, so the possibility of getting more volunteers made the whole plan much more feasible.

Sophie posed the question everyone wanted to ask but feared to, in case Bill thought them not dedicated to bird watching sufficiently to be in a bird club. 'How will we know what to look for? I don't think I've ever seen a falcon before, let alone a rare one.' Everyone concurred and Shelia replied, 'Don't worry about that I will print out some coloured images of both the peregrine, and gyrfalcon, and Bill will add a few helpful notes to help you with your identification.' Bill added, 'The important thing will be to let the other watch stations know if you think you've seen it, and if possible get someone else to confirm what has been seen, better still a photo.'

Bill would make arrangements for members to set up their watching stations in designated locations and would give final instructions on the Saturday morning at 7 am. Mrs Bottomly and Mrs Slater made it clear they might not quite make it at that time, but Bill said he would leave a note on his front door for late comers with instructions where to go to and what to do. Felicity promised to come early with as many volunteers as she could muster.

Chapter 4

The Clutterbucks call in the Archaeologists

Nigel and Julie Clutterbuck were having afternoon tea in their conservatory on a lovely sunny spring day; talking about the Annual Church Spring Fete and Garden Competition which was shortly due to take place. 'What about you entering our garden in this years competition, you said you would last year but put it off, remember,' suggested Nigel. They both looked out across their large lawn, which Nigel had given its first cut of the season earlier that day. 'Well actually I don't really want to do that, I think its important that the villagers with small gardens should be encouraged to enter it, I think with our beautiful garden they might be a bit perturbed, and imagine if we didn't get an award!' she continued, 'And you know how unpopular Mrs Bottomly was at winning again last year.' Nigel nodded he could see her point, but it would be nice to get an award.

Julie concentrated her looks and said, 'Actually Nigel we need to talk about the garden anyway.' Nigel looked up, 'What about the garden dear?' "Well you remember the bones in the flower bed last year, and my seeing a monk a few weeks ago,' said Julie. 'Yes, what about it?' replied Nigel. 'Well I haven't told you something,' she said. 'What haven't you told me,' quizzed Nigel. She went on to tell Nigel all about her lunchtime spent with Enid, and their discussing Alf's sighting of a monk in the dunes. She told him about Enid explaining to her, that the early monks probably had wives and children. That it was possible that the Vikings slaughtered all of them that may have lived in the Uppbury Priory at the time, as Enid's research findings from last year suggested. Nigel responded, 'Well I had thought of that, but you got so upset last year when you uncovered those bones and especially the child's skull I decided it was better to let sleeping dogs lie.'

After some discussion the Clutterbuck's decided that the bones in their garden had to be investigated, but before they called the police, Nigel rang the Lincoln Museum. 'Could you put me through to Zoe Hartington please?' 'Could you tell me what its about please?' asked the receptionist. 'Sorry I can't but if you give her my name I'm sure she'll want to talk.' 'Can you give me your name then Sir?' asked the receptionist. 'Clutterbuck, Dr Clutterbuck,' he almost yelled down the phone whilst trying to keep his cool.

'Nigel how nice to hear from you, not more Viking bones or things is it?' asked a cheerful Zoe. Nigel explained the situation, but hinted they had only very recently found some bones, not wanting to let her know he had kept quiet for months about them. Zoe agreed to come down at the weekend to have a peek, she asked him if he would mind inviting young Sophie Weatherspoon along as well, could be good to encourage her interest since Zoe had decided to take young Sophie under her wing, and wanted an excuse to talk to her parents anyway about her career prospects and make it clear that archaeologists rarely got long term employment and could be out of work for months sometimes, years just like actors.

Alf Prichard called in at the Rectory to collect the leaflets that Julie had typed up for the Melton-Uppbury Historical Group, he had promised to hand deliver them to all their local members. Gerald Parker was taking some to deliver them to the groups Reedstorpe members where he worked:

The Melton-Uppbury Historical Group Summer Programme

Saturday the 15th of June: Visit to Flag Fen cost person £8 includes bus and entrance fees. Take a packed lunch meet at Rectory 9 am sharp

Saturday the 10th of July: Visit Lincoln Museum Behind the scenes with Zoe Lake. Free entry. Sharing cars meet 10 am at the Rectory. Tea and biscuits provided free.

Saturday the 12th of August: Day trip to the British Museum Bus cost £12 per person, no entrance fees. Meet at Rectory prompt 8 am. Take packed lunch or use museums cafeteria.

Saturday the 11th of Sept: Visit the Sutton Hoo Heritage Site. Fee £5 per person bus cost, entrance fees if any extra. Take packed lunch. Meet at Rectory 10 am.

'Come in Alf the leaflets are on the kitchen table I think, would you like a beer while you're here?' 'Oh yes please Dr Clutterbuck very kind of you.' Nigel led Alf out into the conservatory, and said; 'Actually I was wondering if you would like to run your metal detector over my garden if you can spare the time?' avoiding the question of bones, and intending to keep any metal detecting Alf might undertake well away from the flower borders. 'Do you think there might be anything in it?' posed Alf. 'Probably not, but you never know might be the odd Victorian garden implement, I'm just curious really, who knows what we might be walking on.' 'Okay I will come over tomorrow first thing, if that's all right, fifty-fifty if there is anything of value,' offered Alf. They agreed, Nigel told Alf not to make too much noise if he was there before 8.30 since he was not an early riser these days. And asked him to concentrate his metal detecting to the lawns and shrubbery at the front of the house.

The Museum Archaeologist Arrives

Saturday morning arrived and Zoe Hartington nee Lake; drove into the Rectory Drive, she was greeted by Julie and Nigel Clutterbuck on the front door steps. It was the first time they had met up since last year, and they were all very pleased to get re-acquainted. Julie grabbed Zoe's arm and led her into the kitchen. 'Well Zoe we are so glad you could come, we are in a bit of a dilemma actually,' she said as she poured out a cup of tea, and offered Zoe a cup cake. 'Nigel said something about bones in your garden,' Zoe said. 'Yes that's it,' Julie said, and blurted out the truth of how she found the bones last year, she just couldn't look Zoe in the eye and pretend they had only just found them, as she and Nigel had planned to do.

Zoe was kneeling down carefully examining a few bones that Nigel had uncovered, by removing some of the turf he had relayed last year, after Julies fright. Using her trowel she gently exposed the partial skull of a child, after ten minutes or so she had exposed a number of bones, some possibly children's but also adults. They were blackened with age and Zoe guessed they must be at least a few hundred years old. 'Well Nigel I'm afraid you will have to call the police, but don't worry I can certainly verify these are greatly aged bones, so they won't be bothered but they will have to come and have a peek.

Shelia went back to the house and called out the local constable based at Reedsthorpe, he arrived within the hour and took a statement from Dr Clutterbuck about the find. No mention of when they found the bones, the constable just assumed they had only just been found. Zoe gave a brief statement verifying the possible age of the bones subject to a laboratory examination and carbon 14 tests, and he went away happy to report to his superiors. Zoe and the Clutterbucks re-covered the bones, excepting the partial child's skull, which Zoe carefully wrapped up to take back to the museum.

In the Rectory conservatory they discussed the next step, clearly an excavation had to be carried out, but unlike the last one on the beach, this was to be in the Clutterbuck's own garden. Zoe made it clear to Nigel and Julie that as the landowners the ball was in their court, they could agree to a dig, or in fact forbid it. 'But it a great opportunity, to see if there's any evidence that these were monks, and as

Julie said it would explain the recent sightings, also of course we could allow your Historical Group to become fully involved.' Nigel said, 'I suppose your right it's a great opportunity, a dig in our own grounds the chance for us all to get involved.' Julie added, 'And of course young Sophie would be really pleased to get some more hands on experience.' Nigel turning to his wife said, 'Well in the end Julie it's your decision, I don't want you getting upset with it all, remember how you were when you first found the bones, last year.'

After some debate Julie made it clear if it was the monks and their families, she wanted to see them properly buried in the church graveyard, there had to be closure for the poor monks or whoever they were. Zoe said she would be happy for Nigel to act as her second in command on the excavation since Mick her husband and fellow archaeologist had not been able to work with her since they had got married; he was working down near Boston on a big excavation.

Zoe left for Lincoln intending to go straight to her museum office, to start working out when and how the excavation should be organised. As she drove home she wondered if Dorothy the mature theology student she had become friends with after the events of last year in Melton-Uppbury would like to get involved after all it was going to be a churchy type dig.

Dorothy was just about to read yet another treatise on Martin Luther when the phone rang out. 'Hi is that you Dorothy,' called out the familiar cheery voice of Zoe. 'Yes of course it is! Who else is going to answer my mobile you daft thing, there's only me in this squat little room, student quarters aren't meant for entertaining visitors,' she said laughing. Zoe went on to invite Dorothy out for a couple of early evening drinks in the Grapes, a pub situated about half way between the museum and Dorothy's Theological College.

'I've some exciting news about the monks at Melton and I could do with your help if any more research is needed.' Dorothy threw down her book which she was still half reading whilst speaking to Zoe, and yelped, 'Thank God for that, I've got to get out of here for a while, really sick of Martin Luther and his monotonous tracts.'

They met at the Grapes, a small but very old fashioned public house, with a tiny bar and original oak beams as arranged, and Zoe was able to update Dorothy about the recent re-occurrences of monk sightings and the bones in the Clutterbuck's garden. 'What has Rosemary said about it all?' exclaimed Dorothy. 'I don't think she knows about the bones, but it appears everybody knows about the monks appearance in the dunes again, because it was Alf Pritchard who saw it,' Zoe said. 'Right, I'll ring her when I get home, I was thinking about going over to stay with her for a couple of days next week anyway,' Dorothy said. After a pleasant couple of hours they both departed from the pub, Dorothy headed back to her College Digs and Zoe started the climb up the hill to the small terraced house she and her husband Mick rented near the Cathedral. Zoe had married Mick last year after they got together working on the Viking Dig at Melton-

Uppbury and the Rev Rosemary Fitter had presided over the service at St Guthlac's.

Chapter 5

Rare Bird Sighting Confirmed

Saturday morning Bill and Shelia were busy printing out a few extra copies of images of peregrine and gyrfalcons, when Felicity drove into their close with a car full off excited nursing friends. She had a night out with them on the Thursday night, and in the course of general conversation gently hinted that she was looking forward to seeing a rare bird on the Saturday, and if any one else was interested she might be able to let them come along. Her friend Martha a single mother of a teenage boy, asked if she could bring him along. Felicity said that should be okay, and that started the ball rolling. She soon had five volunteers. Shelia led the first of Felicity's friends to the mini bus as Felicity yelled out, 'Back in about fifteen minutes got to nip back and collect Martha and her lad.'

Bill had a rough rota worked out but not knowing who was free at any particular time found it almost impossible to actually get it into motion. Shelia said, 'For heavens sake Bill forget your list lets just get one person settled at each site then work out how we can rotate things about.' 'Okay I don't suppose there's much choice really.' As he was handing out the identification pictures to the nurses sitting in the mini bus, Geoffrey and Mrs Bottomly arrived. Geoffrey's face lit up when he saw all the girls giggling and smiling at him. Mrs Slater came into the Close puffing and panting, followed by young Sophie who was not so pleased to see a gang of young giggling women carrying on with Geoffrey. They boarded the bus and Sophie grabbed Geoffrey's hand and said, 'You had better, sit with me, I want you to explain exactly what we are looking for.' Geoffrey blushed looked forlornly back at the girls as he did as he was told.

Bill yelled to Shelia as he was driving the mini-bus out of the bungalows drive, 'Wait here for Felicity will you, I'll be back as soon as I've got these settled.' First stop the Inn: Col James had managed to borrow five small tents from a friend of his in the TA after Shelia had spoken to him about the need for their members to camp out for a day or so.

Bill parked up in the pub car park. James met them and got the volunteers to put four of the tents on the mini-bus. He then led, all the group members to the first designated watching site not far from the pub, designated as number 1 by the Rookery, overlooking the river and fenlands in a westerly direction. There he demonstrated how the tents had to be erected. Bill got Mrs Bottomly and Mrs Slater to look after this station since if they had any problems it was only a few minutes walk back to the pub. Mrs Bottomly had forgotten her binoculars but Mrs Slater had hers, Bill made sure they had the pictures and a mobile phone to report any sightings. Next stop St Guthlac's Church, from which site number 2 had to be walked to, via the riverside track. Bill sent Geoffrey and one of the nurses called Margaret down there, since Geoffrey could carry the tent, which was far from light weight. The third site number 3 was situated at the western end of the graveyard; here he left Sophie and nurse Janet to organise them selves. Slowly the watch stations were set up, Bill returned home to organise Felicity; her friend Nurse Martha and her stroppy son, who clearly was not best pleased at being pulled out of his bed at such an unearthly hour on a Saturday morning.

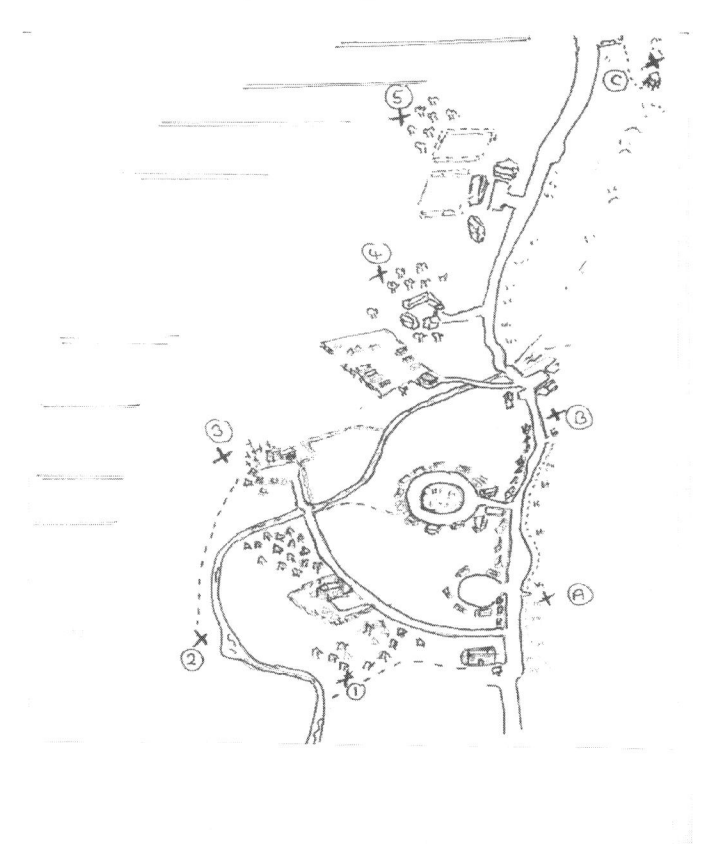

Bills Gyrfalcon Watching Stations Plan

Having got at least one or two volunteers at each of the observation stations Bill wrote down who was where and tried to work out how he could monitor the situation:

Bird Watching Station Volunteers Saturday 8.30AM

Fenland Watching Stations/

Station No 1: Mrs Slater and Mrs Bottomly (Tented at the edge of the Rookery on the east bank of the river).

Station No 2: Geoffrey Thompson and Nurse Margaret (Tented on the west bank of the river).

Station No 3: Sophie Weatherspoon and Nurse Janet (Tented at the edge of the churchyard).

Station No 4: Nurse Emma (Tented in the woods behind Home farm).

Station No 5: Sidney Harding (Tented behind the riding stables wood).

Coast Watching Stations/

Station A: Shelia Taylor (On the Dunes but just a few yards from her home).

Station B: Nurse Martha and son Tony (In the Café overlooking the beach and sea).

Station C: Felicity Oundle (In the Reserve Hide).

Bill decided to do an hourly stint himself at each of the stations, allowing those who were stationed there to go home or take a break. Each of the sites had at least one pair of binoculars, fortunately Bill had quite a few spare pairs, it was his 'want' to buy the latest recommended models much to the indignation of his long suffering wife, a pocket book of British Birds and his photocopy images of peregrines and gyrfalcons.

All the volunteers had been asked to bring packed lunches and flasks of tea or coffee, so no one should be hungry or dying of thirst. James at the pub had agreed to put on a buffet for them at 7 pm when Bill intended to call off the days watch. All the volunteers were to keep a list of all the birds they saw, or at least a description of what they had seen. As the day went on Bill agreed that the volunteers could circulate between the watch stations providing no site was left unmanned.

The nurses in the main had a very good day; even stroppy young Tony got excited at times trying to identify passing sea birds and waders on the beech at low tide. His mother Martha hoped today might stimulate his interests into other directions than just sleeping and his I Pad thing, apart from which their Hide being a café couldn't be better, and a teenage boy eating sweets and ice cream made bird watching a doddle. But even here Tony seemed to be spending an awful lot of time on his mobile phone.

Bill did the rounds, everyone got a break and each observation station bird ticklist got bigger as the day wore on but no falcons, by the time Bill had decided it was late enough to call it a day and get every one back to the Crows Roost for their buffet and drinks it was nearly 7 pm, he was just calling Sidney Harding at station 5 which was at the northern most station to tell him to pack up and collect Nurse Emma from station 4, and reminding them to bring everything of value back and securing the tents, when Sidney yelled 'Hang on Bill something's happening Emma's waving.' With that the phone went dead. Sidney immediately raced down to where Emma was standing; he was well puffed out by the time he reached her. 'Didn't you see it,' she yelled at him 'See what,' asked Sidney sitting on the grass to get his breath back. 'The falcon,' she said. 'What falcon?' he protested. 'The one that I was pointing at that passed your tent, ten minutes ago, why do you think I was waving,' Emma yelled excitedly. Sidney quickly realised that he must have been answering Bills call at the exact moment the bird must have passed him.

The Days events Revealed

Back at the Crows Roost the excited Priory Birders and the volunteers Felicity had recruited from the hospital were exchanging details about the events of the day. Most of the day had been fairly mundane; the biggest excitement for Mrs Bottomly and Mrs Slater who had been based at station 1 by the river had been several sighting of a kingfisher. It was Mrs Slater who saw it first, since there had been a couple nesting in the riverbank near her caravan site last year, the flash of blue was, but a blur; but it could be nothing else.

Their patience was rewarded when they spotted one sitting on a branch overhanging the river on the other bank later that day. All the sites overlooking the fens reported seeing Herons, Crows and Rooks, Mallard, Coots an occasional Kestrel, Little Grebe, or Dab Chick, Curlew and lots of Black Headed gulls. There were many more but Bill was more interested in the falcon sighting.

It transpired that as dusk was descending on them, and all the volunteers were eagerly waiting for Bill to call them to return to the pub, that Geoffrey and nurse Margaret at station 2 noticed a bird of prey sitting on a mound some distance away across the fenland. Geoffrey tried to focus his binoculars on it, but he thought it was a Barn Owl, which would have not been an unexpected sighting at this time of night. But all of a sudden Margaret saw a small bird flying by the bird of prey and heading towards them.

Geoffrey was startled when the whitish bird he was watching suddenly rose up and started flying low towards them at speed, he soon saw the small bird that Margaret was pointing at flying fast just in front of the big bird but very close to ground level, suddenly the small bird swerved northwards along the edge of the river, as it did so Geoffrey got a good view of the falcon like shape of its pursuer, it was almost wholly white with curved wings heading up past the church. He shouted to Margaret, 'Quick phone station 3 tell them to watch out for the birds passing if they get that far.' Margaret rang. Sophie answered, 'We can see the white falcon it's passing us just now, it looks like the gyrfalcon in the picture.' Sophie's partner nurse Janet rang her friend Emma at station 4 and told her to try and get a photo, she had one of these new 50 times zoom jobs.

Emma saw the white bird flying fast and low towards her, but she couldn't see what it was chasing, she started taking continuous photos, trying to aim the camera at the white bird. She was still trying to taking pictures as she waved to Sidney who she could see was on the phone not taking any notice of what was happening in front of him. She watched in dismay as the bird and its prey vanished northwards right under Sidney's nose.

'Well lets have a look at your photos then', demanded Bill of Emma excitedly. 'Oh yes in all the excitement and rushing back here I forgot about them,' cried Emma. She pulled her digital camera from her bag and switched it on. Bill, Shelia, and Sidney crowded round her as she looked at the screen and slowly ran through the shots she had taken. Most of them were blurred since it had been impossible to press the focus button for each shot, she had managed to focus the camera for one shot just as the bird flew by her station, and this was the only identifiable one she had been able to get.

Emma's one clear Photo shoot of the Gyrfalcon

Bill looked the small image on the camera, being small it wasn't able to be sure but he was very excited as he cried out; 'It's definitely not a peregrine, come on Emma lets get this image on my computer and we will get a print out of it.' Bills bungalow was only a few hundred yards from the pub, so Emma and Bill were back in no time.

Everyone of the birders and other locals crowded round the table where Bill had placed the A4 photo next to his old photo, copies of which they had all been using at their watching stations during the day. There was no doubt it was a gyrfalcon, but much lighter, almost white rather than Bills old picture which was a Norwegian gyrfalcon and somewhat darker. 'So it looks like young Geoffrey has found an Icelandic Gyrfalcon a rare visitor indeed to these shores,' said Sidney reading through the details of variant gyrfalcons that were vagrant visitors to the United Kingdom, in his bird book.

Chapter 6

Archaeologists Dig Up The Rectory Garden

The morning of the dig Zoe arrived accompanied by a couple of Museum volunteers; they unloaded their gear onto the Rectory Drive. Firstly she got John one of the young volunteers to take a few photos of the area they were going to dig in.

Young Sophie Weatherspoon arrived as they were unloading, Dr Clutterbuck having called her at the request of Zoe last night. She was keen as mustard. A little earlier she had raced down the stairs of her flat into the shop, grabbing a couple of mars bars as she did so off the shelf, 'Sorry mum can't stop got to get to the Rectory, Zoe will be waiting for me.' Her mum Kate was busy sorting the morning papers and getting ready to open up their post office counter. 'Typical!' she declared, 'Not a word, just bounce out without a care in the world, I wondered who she was on the phone to last night,' yelled Kate. Kate needed to nip into Reesdsthorpe to get the weeks shopping, they might own a little shop but they like everyone else had to get their main shopping from a supermarket, the trouble was she had hoped Sophie would mind the shop while she was out, since her husband Harry had gone to the big cash and carry at Louth so wouldn't be back till lunch time.

As the team got to work setting out the gear and measuring up possible excavation test pit sites, Dr Clutterbuck brought out some spades and rakes, and a couple of hand brushes. Zoe had a chat with her two experienced digger volunteers and set Sophie to working with them. The first job was to mark out a 2x3 metre plot where Julie Clutterbuck had exposed the bones last year. The plot marked out, they set to removing the turf and barrowing it to the far corner of the garden. Some bones were showing directly below the turf level since Zoe and Nigel had only, lightly laid the turf back down when Zoe had been called in by the Clutterbuck's a couple of weeks previously.

Zoe then got out the drawing board, which had a large graph lined sheet of waterproof, tracing paper securely attached to it. The diggers slowly and carefully started to gently brush the soil away from the bones gradually exposing more as they gently used their trowels. John was showing Sophie what to do, both on their hands and knees working away in tandem. John was twenty two, and had been going out as a volunteer on digs since he was eighteen, but it was the first time he had been teaching an attractive girl like Sophie about archaeology. He couldn't help but notice her long black hair, cute pretty face, slim build, and wearing a tight T Shirt top, and tight jeans. She too was a little attracted to this young man at her side, who was pretty good looking, in fact very good looking she thought compared to Geoffrey who for all she was attracted to him, and was supposed to be his girlfriend was still a bit of a geek, but a loveable geek.

Dr Clutterbuck brought the fold up garden chair from his conservatory and set it by the side of the newly exposed excavation area. Zoe passed him the drawing board, and he began to fill in the graph paper outlining the 2x3 metre area. He had to keep standing over the dig to get a plan view of it. There were bones partially exposed by the diggers, and he had to draw them as nearly exactly as he could into the correct squares. 'Ah Nigel I can see you've remembered how to do it then,' said Zoe peering over his shoulders. Dr Clutterbuck had done most archaeological site jobs in the past, whilst studying the subject part time at University, but had confessed to Zoe he was a little bit older and doddery now. 'Yes Zoe its all coming back now,' he said quite pleased with himself. 'Good,' she replied, 'I've got to go back to the museum now to take some of these bones, and get some more boxes to put the rest of finds in, so can you get John and Lewis (who was the second volunteer) to start removing the turf for the second test area by the other hedge, and when you've finished drawing this layer, start going down a bit more to expose more of the bones with Sophie, she seems to have got the knack of it already.'

As Zoe drove out of the drive, Julie Clutterbuck came down the garden path carrying a tray of tea and home made scones. 'Right everyone,' cried out Nigel with a new air of authority, 'Break off from what you are doing and enjoy some of my wife's freshly made scones.' Sophie sidled up to Julie and whispered, 'This is great Mrs Clutterbuck, my second archaeological dig, and decent talent as well,' glancing over at John as she did so.

Mrs Clutterbuck gave Sophie a friendly wink and whispered, 'And what about poor Geoffrey then is he history now?' 'Oh Mrs C I'm only young, got to look around, you know, trying to get a place on an archaeology course is my main preoccupation but one has to have a pastime, long as dad doesn't find out,' even so Sophie felt a little guilty being reminded of Geoffrey's adoration of her.

Julie Clutterbuck collected up the mugs and Nigel's special china teacup, the only cup he liked having his tea in, and carried the tray back to the house with a big smile on her face.

Julie tried to remember what it was like to be a teenager again, but could only remember getting old before her time. She had left home at eighteen to go to Huddersfield Physiotherapy College, and didn't really get the chance to enjoy conventional University Student Life, since her Dad had died when she was fifteen, and her mum had gone to pieces, and as the only child she had taken on the role of mother. She was forever travelling to and fro from her home in Reedsthorpe and the college at Huddersfield. Her mother did after a few years get back a bit of her old self, but she never fully recovered from her loss, sadly for Julie there was no one to help her over the loss of her Dad.

In a way getting married to Nigel, who was quite a bit older than her, and helping run his medical practice in Reedsthorpe really helped repair some of the wounds she had suffered. In a way Nigel had replaced her Dad and he was able to help a lot with her mother. Julie envied Sophie and the opportunities life appeared to be offering her, but she was extremely fond of her, as was Nigel. Sophie had spent quite a lot of time over the last few months pouring over Nigel's history and archaeology books in his small library. Julie herself although interested in those subjects, couldn't build up the passion that Nigel had for them, but she was very happy to see he could share his interests with young Zoe.

Extra Help on the Dig

Rosemary and her friend Dorothy arrived at the Rectory late on a Friday evening on the second day of the Clutterbuck Dig. Rosemary had invited Dorothy to spend the weekend with her in her church flat in Reedsthorpe, after Dorothy had updated her about the impending dig that Zoe had told her about a couple of weeks ago.

Rosemary's church flat was to be vacated by the end of the month, since she was no longer responsible for St Georges or the other churches she had ministered too prior to the recent changes. She might have a job, but accommodation was a sore point at the moment. The Diocesan appointed new priest for St Georges was desperate to get into the flat, so Rosemary's quest for a new home preferably in Melton-Uppbury was becoming urgent.

Rosemary was quite excited about the possibility of these bones being that of the monks of the Saxon Priory. She knew about the more recent monk sightings, that of Julie's hence the present garden excavation, and of Alf Pritchard's on the dunes. She was sure these apparitions were the monks appealing for a proper Christian burial in consecrated ground.

Last year the monks apparition appearing in the church had led Dorothy and Rosemary to the monastic hoard that saved St Guthlac's Church from being closed down, better than that, the money that had saved the church also gave Rosemary, her new role as the Rector of St Guthlac's at the insistence of Col James Smith-Fitzroy the rightful owner of the treasure.

Rosemary was basically now her own boss, very much like the olden days when rich families like the predecessors of her benefactor James, the Fitzroy family employed usually a member of their own family to look after the spiritual welfare of the family ensuring that the leading members of the family were to be assured a place in heaven. If anything she was now under-employed, quite a reversal of her former role as Diocesan appointed priest to three parish churches plus, one of which was St Guthlac's.

One of the things she really missed about her former role was the feeling of pride she always got when she entered St George's Church in Reedsthorpe, St Georges was a cathedral like building with an air of historicity, and she knew that as its Vicar she was listed as its very first lady priest, and as such her name had been entered on the brass scroll of former incumbents to the post going back to 1189.

On their way to the Rectory, Rosemary had stopped off at the Weatherspoons Post Office cum General Store and Newsagent, where she left a post card with Kate Weatherspoon to put in her shop window:

Youngish Professional Lady seeks self-contained one bed roomed accommodation in Village. References available. Reasonable Rent Paid in Advance. Tele: 77089246.

'Could be difficult accommodations a bit scarce round here as you well know, Rosemary,' said Kate.

The Rev Rosemary Fitters last base Church St Georges in Reedsthorpe

Julie Clutterbuck was as usual wearing her thick white polo necked knitted jumper, and baggy jeans, as she ushered them both into the kitchen for tea. The Rectory was an old building, where signs of damp and disrepair occasionally showed themselves, although cleverly disguised by Julie, with curtains and drapes, ornaments and old fashioned pictures, even in summer many of the rooms were cold.

The Clutterbuck's although reasonably well off, Nigel as a retired GP, but they had never put any money away, and the problems that basically forced him to sell up their practice, meant they made little on the deal. So it was a case of make do and mend. Julie was contented if she got her yearly week or two boating on the Norfolk Broads, the rest of her time was consumed in voluntary work.

Nigel's time was spent on his Melton-Uppbury Historical Group, organising this or that, visiting historic sites and museums and doing a little archaeological writing. But this dig on his own doorstep, with him co-directing was for him a source of great pleasure, he foresaw himself writing a book about the excavation and the recovery of the bones of the mutilated corpses of the Saxon monks and their families.

Julie gave the younger women a hug, she was fond of both of them despite the age gap of twenty to thirty years they all had a similar outlook on life, although Julie found some of her younger friends opinions a little far out for herself. She never believed the day would come when a female priest would preside at Church of England church services let alone become one of her closest friends.

Having finished their women's gossip catch up over tea and cake, Julie led them through to the conservatory where Nigel was sorting out a few trays of archaeological finds. He was as usual in his old and battered linen suit, with a glass of whiskey in one hand and a piece of pot in the other, almost dropping both as the girls entered, he rose from his chair to greet them, another round of friendly hugs before they all were seated. 'Well come on Nigel spill the beans, what have you dug up?' asked Dorothy. Julie spouted up, 'Not a lot by all accounts, isn't that so Nigel.' 'Far from it Dorothy, take no notice of Julie, dead people don't really get her very excited, do they dear,' as he fondly looked across at her. He drew their attention to the trays on the coffee table. He extracted a few pieces of flint, which were clearly not connected with Saxon monks, and some Roman pottery.

As Nigel explained these finds are normal but out of context, they were found at the same level as some of the bones, which meant dating might be a problem. 'What do you mean out of context?' asked Rosemary a bit bewildered. Dorothy interjected, 'It means that the layers of earth or soil have been mixed up, doesn't it Nigel.' 'Yes quite right Dorothy, basically the flints are from the pre-history period, the roman pottery of course comes from the first to forth century, and we think the bones are from the sixth to eighth centuries, so some how or other they have all got mixed together, the lower soil levels with the more recent ones which would have been above them.'

Nigel explained that this was only what they found in the second test plot, along with a number of bones that Zoe had boxed up for the museum. The first excavation plot was where Julie uncovered some bones last year, they were in context, and so far they had recovered the bones from three Adults, and a child and a baby. All had evidence of being seriously hacked at, possibly at the time of death or possibly afterwards.

There was still a lot more careful excavation to be done, Zoe estimated another week or so at least. 'So what's your plans for tomorrow Nigel,' asked

Rosemary. 'We carry on,' 'Who's we?' asked Dorothy. Nigel replied, 'Well young Sophie, and two young chaps, volunteers from the museum I think, and Zoe and myself of course.' 'Zoe won't be here,' interrupted Julie, 'She's just rung to say she's going to Cambridge with the bones, the lab people are apparently very excited about it, the staff there are going into work especially to examine them, even though its out of normal working hours.

Dorothy and Rosemary looked at each other, and Dorothy asked, 'Nigel would another couple of volunteers be appreciated,' with a pleading expression on her face. 'Why yes, you two are young enough to do some digging, I'm too old for the heavy stuff now, to be honest I can't even kneel down for long.' So it was sorted Nigel would now have charge of the excavation, with a staff of five keen and enthusiastic volunteers.

After Rosemary and Dorothy had driven off back to Reedsthorpe, Nigel sat down to plan out what he had to do tomorrow. With extra help he could now open another trench, so he would have Sophie and John continuing the first important plot, exposing more of the bones that appeared to have been piled up on top of each other. He would get the other museum volunteer, along with Rosemary and Dorothy to open up a new 3x5 trench, apart from the trench Zoe asked him to get started before she left.

The next afternoon Julie took a call from Zoe in Cambridge, 'Exciting news Julie but I think I'd better tell your husband first.' 'Yes I think you'd better, hold on a moment,' Julie said as she wandered though to the conservatory with their cordless phone, and out onto the veranda. 'Nigel, Zoe's on the phone, come on she wants to speak to you.' 'Hello Nigel the news confirms our thoughts, the bones are circ 800 and the cuts and incisions we saw on them appear to have been done by double edged swords, and some form of axe. The evidence suggests the victims were alive at the time when these terrible injuries were inflicted upon them.' Nigel tried to take in this appalling but exciting news, 'What about the child's skull?' he quietly asked. 'Pretty awful, I'm afraid the poor kid was decapitated, one blow by the look of it, he was only about five years old they think.' Nigel stood back and handed Julie the phone as the tears started to trickle down his face. Julie spoke to Zoe, 'Sorry Zoe, Nigel's a bit unwell, afraid I'll have to let you go for now, when are you coming back?' 'Give him my love, sorry if the news has upset him, I'll be back about lunch time tomorrow, staying over tonight in case they find anything else out, the lab boys and girls are working till the jobs finished apparently, bye for now.'

Nigel was sat in his conservatory chair, looking graven and ashen, the tears were still welling up in his eyes, as he imaged the horror of the Viking whom only last year they gave a Viking funeral to, slicing off the head of that poor defenceless child in cold blood. Julie knew in this type of mood it was best to leave him to it, to allow his mind to accommodate this horrific information whatever it was. At the time she had no idea what Zoe had told her husband, but guessed it meant these poor people had suffered a terrible death, she had shuddered thinking about the possibilities.

She went out to the diggers and told them to pack up, explaining that Nigel was a little unwell but they could all carry on in the morning, all but Rosemary of course who had the Sunday Morning service at St Guthlac's to conduct. Sophie, John, and the other young man Lewis from the museum headed off to the Crows Roost Inn. The boys had been allowed to camp in the Clutterbuck's garden whilst the dig was on, so the short walk to the pub was a pleasing thought especially for John who was really getting close to Sophie, or so he thought.

Julie took Rosemary and Dorothy round to the front of the house avoiding the conservatory where Nigel sat in a melancholy mood; using the front door and settling them in the kitchen for a coffee and a few home made oatcakes. They chatted about many subjects but tried to avoid the one thing they wanted to talk about, Zoe's phone call, in case Nigel came in while they were talking.

Julie however did in due course tell them what she thought the phone call was about; and tried to explain how Nigel always took death badly, he had got much worse in the last few years, since he still held himself responsible for Enid Barrhead's husbands death, due to him making a misdiagnosis of Roland's condition despite the coroners verdict of misadventure. Enid never held him responsible, but the loss of his friend weighed heavily on his soul and in his heart. Life was a precious thing, and the death of a five year old even over a thousand years ago was upsetting.

Sophie Causes a Stir

At the Crows Roost Inn Enid Barrhead was having a gin and tonic, with beloved pooch Truffles sitting at her feet. She was sharing a table with Jack Wilkinson from the Reedsthorpe Museum who had earlier visited the Clutterbuck's to get the latest on the excavation, and was telling her what developments had taken place. Edith was a member of The Melton-Uppbury historical Group set up by Gerald Parker and Nigel Clutterbuck last year, as Jack was the group's Museum Contact he was always up to date with the groups affairs even though he lived in Reedsthorpe. Len the church Sexton was in his usual corner near the bar, talking to the landlord Col James.

Geoffrey Thompson was with his dad at the other end of the bar, when Sophie Weatherspoon flounced in, with two strange young men one on each arm. 'Two pints of your best Ale landlord, please and whatever this beautiful young lady wants,' called out John. 'Right young Sir that'll be two pints of 'Pigstrotters' and a double Bacardi and coke,' replied James as he poured out two pints and a coke for Sophie. 'That will be ten pounds forty, young Sir,' he said with a big grin on his face. John went as red as a beetroot as he tried to empty his pockets of loose change and counted out five pounds and ten pence. Geoffrey in the background had really got angry when the three of them entered the bar, but as the scene unfolded, and a shamed John didn't have enough money to pay for the round he had just ordered, Geoffrey smiled, and

Sophie started to giggle, as Col James roared with laughter and cried out, 'We don't have any underage drinking here no matter how beautiful a gal might be,' handing Sophie her coke and taking five pounds from the pile of change John had put on the bar. Everyone round the bar started to join in the giggling and laughter. Geoffrey couldn't resist getting a dig in, as he sidled up to Sophie who by now was sitting down on a sofa seat between the two boys. 'Give me a nod Sophie when your ready for another coke, I might just be able to afford that, but keep off the Bacardi and coke bit pricey that.' She smiled as she realised he had been jealous of her new friends.

Enid on her way out with Truffles, stopped by the sofa Sophie was sitting on and said, 'That's right Sophie you keep them on their toes, make sure they know your very choosy who you socialise with, it's the best way you know.' A big smile cracked out from her previously stern face, as she turned away from the sofa and headed for the door.

'Hell do you know everybody in this place,' asked John's friend Lewis. 'Yes I guess I do,' she said, smiling coyly. 'And do they all keep an eye out for you, like check out who you go out with and such like,' said John looking down in the mouth. 'Of course, they all know what my Dad would do if any one took advantage of me,' she teased. 'And I wont be taking up your kind offer of sleeping in your tent tonight, perhaps another night if my Dad says I can,' with that she flounced out of the pub just as she had come in just a short while ago, and headed for home alone as she had planned.

Chapter 7

The Twitchers Invasion

The Priory Birders had a really exciting night at the pub, the sighting of the gyrfalcon was what they all wanted to see, but no one actually thought anyone would be lucky enough to do so, and Emma's photo was a scoop for the group. The next thing however was to try and see if it was just hunting in this area or passing through. As Bill had pointed out there had been several other sightings mainly up around the river Humber.

Early next morning everyone headed off to their watching stations, Bill had got everyone to change around so that no one would get too bored with their fairly basic environment, which in most cases was quite cramped, two people squeezing in a small mountain tent meant for one was a bit too much for some of them. However yesterday it had certainly pleased Geoffrey finding himself squeezed in a tent with nurse Margaret who was very attractive, and wore a scent that was almost intoxicating.

Bill was with Margaret at station 2, where yesterday, Geoffrey and Margaret had first spotted the gyrfalcon on a mound. Bill had sent Geoffrey up to the Reserve Hide now station C, where he had made the original sighting, but Geoffrey cursed all morning knowing that Margaret would probably be lying in her tent with just a pair of binoculars for company for most of the day, momentarily forgetting his girlfriend Sophie.

Bill had brought his high-powered x100 telescope and had attached a camera with various adapters so he could take photos through it. 'Right Margaret exactly where did you both first see the bird yesterday?' he asked as they stood at the side of the tent scanning the horizon with their binoculars. The river behind them was ebbing with the tide and quite noisily washing by, making conversation a little difficult at times. Bill repeated his question a bit louder this time. Margaret looked round at him and pointed across the fens to a mound by a dyke in the distance. 'I've got it, hey there's a bird there now!' he exclaimed excitedly. He knelt down to get behind the telescope that he had set up on a small tripod at the tent entrance ready for use later that day.

Bills Digiscope view of the Gyrfalcon

He squeezed himself backwards into the tent not wishing to knock the scope, and switched on the camera. The 2x3 screen lit up and showed an expanse of blurred fenland and sky, until Bill adjusted the scopes focus ring. He carefully pointed the scope in the general direction of the mound that Margaret had pointed out, and slowly located the bird on the mound, carefully refocusing he started rapidly clicking his extendable camera remote switch, Snap, Snap, Snap; whilst doing this he kept gently adjusting the focus trying his best not to knock the tripod.

Margaret was still standing scanning the fens through the old pair of binoculars she had been lent, unaware that the gyrfalcon was there. Bill slowly climbed out of the tent and moved the telescope and tripod further forward so it could now be used outside the tent; he reset everything and refocused on the falcon, which could again be clearly seen on the camera screen. 'Right Margaret get down here and see this,' he gently grabbed her arm and guided her into position.

'That's fantastic,' she declared, 'Why is it just sitting there, is it nesting?' Bill replied 'Afraid not its looking for prey, if it was breeding here it would be a miracle, they always nest on cliffs using the nests of other birds, and never this far south of the arctic circle.' While Margaret was viewing the bird, Bill started to phone round the other stations alerting them to the sighting. Everyone wanted to descend on station 2 to see the bird, but Bill had to warn them off, since any extra activity might well scare the bird off for good. Bill then left Margaret on her own and walked swiftly back to the pub car park, collected his mini-bus and drove the few yards north to the lay by and his watching station A; set up in the dunes with a good view over the beach and sea, he joined Sidney Harding and showed him his most recent photos of the falcon.

It was around twilight when the first signs of trouble started emerging. Bill was just about to ring round the watching stations to get everyone to pack their gear, including tents and wait for him to collect them in his mini-bus, when his mobile phone rang. 'Hello is that you Bill?' 'Oh is that you James, I'm just about to round up the troops. So we'll be at the pub shortly,' answered Bill.

'No that's not what I'm ringing you for, there's about twenty bird watchers just left the pub heading for your tent near the rookery, I've never seen anything like it they all have huge telescopes and huge white telescopic sights and cameras galore. They are all racing down the path, you'd better warn who you have stationed down there that they are on their way. Bill was just about to drive back to the pub, when his phone rang out again.

He pulled into the lay by, James said, 'Bill they are coming back again, some seem to be heading up Church Lane.' As Bill switched off his phone, he had just pulled out of the lay by, heading towards the pub when he saw a dozen so cars racing, with burning tyres out of the Inn car park, up into church lane heading towards the church, the dust blew everywhere and tufts of grass were being strewn everywhere where some drivers had miss-negotiated the grass verge.

Bill slowed down his mini-bus and pulled into the Rectory Drive. Nigel and Julie Clutterbuck were standing at the entrance to the drive looking quite ashen. 'What's going on Bill, that's not your lot is it?' yelled out a furious Mrs Clutterbuck. 'Nothing to do with me but I can guess what's happened,' said Bill pitifully. He was just about to explain that they must be twitchers and had heard about the gyrfalcon, when they heard the roar of car engines accompanied by some motorbikes coming back down the lane at speed. Bill and Julie stood out into the road waving their arms in a frustrated attempt to stop them, but found themselves flattened up against the hedge side covered in dust and dirt. A worried Nigel caught them both by their arms and led them back into the Rectory Drive, stumbling as he did so.

Bills phone started ringing out; his volunteers at stations 1 and 2 had each momentarily been besieged by the mob of twitchers and were desperate to know what was going on. Felicity Oundle was at the reserve Hide station C on her own, when she heard the disturbance. The twitchers had arrived in force at the reserves car park; the sound of roaring engine's and the screeching of brakes scared her almost to death. She opened the Hide door just in time to see all these bird watchers scrambling over the north fence racing towards the headland.

'Mind my scope you idiot!' 'Get out of my way you silly old fool,' was the response. Crash, a ladies telescope slid down a stony embankment. She went sliding down after it, as a teenage boy found himself being trampled underfoot and his binoculars being crushed in the stampede to be the first to get a sighting of the rare Icelandic gyrfalcon.

The Melton Washes Coastal Nature Reserve

Absolute mayhem and chaos had ensued in the car park near the Hide, until things quietened down and Felicity felt brave enough to come out, to see what was going on. She grabbed her kit and headed to where she had parked her car, but it was hemmed in. So she decided to follow the mob up to the headland keeping at a safe distance, by the time she got there most of them were all set up with their telescopic lenses and cameras, looking out to sea, and the scanning the fens to the west. Some of the twitchers looked like the walking wounded from the First World War trenches, after the mob had raced to the headland pushing each other aside in the process. 'What horrible people these are,' she thought to herself, as she took a couple of quick photos of them.

Felicity took this shot of some of the mob

As darkness fell some of the disgruntled birders headed back to the reserve car park. Felicity had phoned Bill who had driven up to collect her. 'Better come back with me, we'll come back to collect your car when these mad heads have gone,' said Bill pointing to a few angry birders who were standing in the car park, who clearly hadn't seen the gyrfalcon. One big man carrying the biggest scope Bill had ever seen, was swaggering down from the headland laughing and carrying on as if he had won the lottery, he was being surrounded by admirers like a pop star, all trying to talk at once. Above the hullabaloo all Felicity and Bill could hear was a very loud voice shouting, 'I got it! I got it! Lets celebrate.'

Pub Besieged

As Bill drove into the Crows Roost Inns car park a few minutes later he and Felicity were faced with the sight of Col James Smith-Fitzroy barring the pubs entrance to a small protesting group of twitchers. Helen one of James barmaids, was standing at the side door only allowing in the locals. Darkness was descending on the scene as the sun finally vanished below the horizon to the west of the village.

A siren was blaring in the distance as the main body of twitchers cars and motorbikes came roaring into the pub car park with their headlights blazing. Cars and bikes were screeching to a halt sending up clouds of dust and grit into the air, a crack was heard as a stone hit a window of the pub, sent up by the tyre of a biker doing a wheelie. The twitching birders all got out of their cars and off their bikes and crowded round the door of the pub, still being barred by James who by this time was being supported by locals. It was becoming an ugly stand off, James knew he couldn't hold this angry mob off for long, he prayed that the police car he could hear was a lot closer than it sounded.

Enid Thwarts the Twitchers

'What the hell do you think you are all doing, make way,' a little elderly lady was forcing her way through the throng of maddened birders waving her umbrella in front of her. A pathway miraculously opened up through the mob as the lady went up to James. 'It's Miss Marple!' cried an isolated voice from the rear of the crowd. 'What's going on James,' she quietly asked. He went on to explain how these assembled birders or twitchers had earlier arrived out of nowhere parking willy nilly all over his car park, and some even tried to drive through the pub garden area leaving a trail of damage. They had then all charged down by the rookery to reach Bills temporary birdwatching station, which overlooked the fenland, smashing down fences to get there, amass. They scared the gyrfalcon off with their noise, and it flew north so they all came back, and stormed off in their vehicles and headed off to the church where Bill had set up another watching station.

They have left a complete trail of destruction everywhere they have been. The dairy herd at Home Farm had to be got back off the main road because these complete idiots, had opened all the farm gates so they could all get up to the other watching stations at the back of the farm and up at the stables.

A furious Edith Barrhead retired village librarian, turned on the crowd still whingeing about their public right to enter the pub. Waving her umbrella in the air, and now joined by young Sophie, her mother Kate, Mrs Alderton and a very angry Mrs Slater who had just been told this lot had been tearing round her caravan park in their cars ripping up the grass, having mistakenly thought it was the entrance to Home Farm.

Edith took the stage, standing directly in front of Col James and the other locals standing up to the mob. Waving her umbrella in the air, she shouted at the crowd of birdwatchers in an authoritarian voice:

'How dare you uncivilised, uncouth, rowdy,

despicable individuals dare call yourselves birdwatchers or twitchers whatever it is you think you are, you are a disgrace to yourselves, your families and more importantly to the bird watching community at large, get back home right now before I poke all of your eyes out with the point of my umbrella.'

She stepped forward pointing her umbrella at the big man, who Bill and Felicity had seen coming down from the Headland on the reserve a little earlier. He stepped back a step or two treading on the toes of those standing up behind him. He saw the point of the umbrella getting closer and closer to his eyes and tumbled back. He was by now certain, that this mad women meant what she said, and he was about to have one of his eyes disgorged. As he fell back everyone behind him started to likewise fall back, one by one they fell until the once threatening mob, found themselves all over the place, clambering over each other to get out of the melee.
A police car screeched to a halt on the main road by the pub blue lights flashing; it could not drive into the car park because there were cars and bikes everywhere, and what appeared to be a mass of bodies disentangling themselves, and apparently being berated by a little old lady with an umbrella. As some of the mob tried to escape by bulldozing their cars out of the car park, the police car moved forward blocking the only entrance in or out. A

period of silence descended on the car park as the two officers got out of their car and walked over to the centre of the recent affray. One of the officers knew James and they stood by the pub door catching up with the events that had led up to this situation. Edith Barrhead was just about to head home, when James called her back, 'Your not going home yet Edith, I owe you a few drinks.' As he said it a cheer went up from the locals, and even some of the beleaguered bird watching mob joined in. The police constable turned and faced the crowd, most of whom were now somewhat subdued and a little contrite:

'Well how are we going to sort this out then, I think first we'll have everyone's name and addresses,' he shouted above the drone of worried voices coming from the crowd.

The Remorseful Twitchers

Gerald Parker Chairman of the Melton-Uppbury Parish Council walked up to James and the police officer, with his note book and pen in hand and said, 'I have been trying to count up the cost of the damage, it's a hell of a lot, none of it can be claimed by insurance because its been caused by mob violence I don't think the insurance companies will cover it. There's damage at the Stables, Home Farm, the Nature Reserve not counting Mrs Slater's, who stood at his side nodding in agreement. 'Well,' said the officer, 'It seems to me this all counts to criminal damage, and that all those who caused it, are going to have to be prosecuted according to law.' The big man stepped forward, 'Look officer there's no need for that I'll pay for any damage,' as he said it he handed the constable a business card:

Joseph Sinclair
Managing Director
Sinclair Electronics
Sinclair House
Mapping
Essex
ES1 2B

0278 99001

'Look when I got the call about the Icelandic Gyrfalcon I got a bit overexcited, never seen one you see, made the mistake of putting it on line where I was going, I invited a few friends to join me but they in turn invited their friends and, well you can see what happened.' The officer turned to Mr Parker and Col Smith-Fitzroy, 'What do you think, I can't really charge all these people, who did what and when it's a nightmare legal situation.' Mr Sinclair piped up, 'Come on gents, take up my offer I'm good for it, look here's £1000 on account,' removing a wad of notes from his fat wallet, 'You can bill me for the rest through my office, handing them another business card.

After some deliberation, Gerald Parker said, 'Give us a few minutes I will have to talk to the owners of the Stables and Home Farm. Ten minutes later after being on the pub phone, Gerald turned to the police officer, 'Right you can go back to Reedsthorpe now constable, we'll sort this out.' James opened the pub doors and told his staff to let everyone in, shouting out in his loudest military voice, 'You can all now come into my pub, but one wrong move or act from any of you and you'll be out on your ears, is that clearly understood.' Gerald led Joseph Sinclair upstairs to James's flat to ratify their agreement and put a few monetary figures together. James and his staff were busy manning the bar and the waitress was run off her feet.

Whilst Gerald and Mr Sinclair were upstairs some of the former mob came up to Mrs Barrhed and the other ladies apologising for the damage and destruction they had done in the village.

The birders asked for a bucket from behind the bar, and the next thing James knew was that a collection was being made as a contribution to Mr Sinclair's commitment. It turned out that a lot of the former hooligan gang of birders were quite wealthy folk, and the total raised; amounted to £1450. 'God,' thought James it's like the Hooray Henrys, rich kids from the City who rampaged London recently, these must be their parents.

Edith was sat in the corner with the Rev Rosemary Fitter who had come to see the progress of the Cluttterbuck's back garden dig, but had been distracted by the melee in the pub car park earlier. Their table was festooned with drinks that they would never ever be able to consume in one sitting, brought over by many of the former mob, who congratulated Edith on her bravery, and said she had really taught them a lesson. Many it appeared had been shocked at their own behaviour, and realised how close they had come to getting a criminal record. Edith elicited many a promise that night, that most of the offenders would start treating each other with more respect and that never again would they trespass on other peoples property doing so much damage.

Bill and the Priory Birders spoke to a lot of the vagrant birders, and tried to fathom out what this compulsion was that drove to such a twitching frenzy. Some of the newer twitchers who had been drawn into the days misdeeds confessed they were very disappointed with the way things developed, and how the poor bird had been scared off, perhaps never to return, and of course only a few of the twitchers actually saw the bird at all.

As Bill said to his group later, 'Fanatics aren't just involved in politics and religion, it's a condition of mankind itself, and fanaticism of any kind in the end destroys the very things it's trying to preserve.'

The Rev Rosemary had no trouble choosing a subject for her next week's sermon that week, and St Guthlac's church was unusually filled to capacity the next Sunday as villagers tried to work out why God had decided to send a plague of birdwatchers upon the village. No one knew who let the cat out of the bag about the gyrfalcon, but Nurse Martha's son Tony was the prime suspect since it was rumoured he had a friend in Reedsthorpe who was suspected to be an egg collector.

As far as the recompense for the damage was concerned Joseph Sinclair was as good as his word, in fact the following day after the event a surveyor arrived in the village, and called on Gerald Parker and asked him to take him round to see the full extent of the damage. 'Right Mr Parker, Mr Sinclair has asked me to apologise for everything that happened, and he's given me the task of ensuring that everything is put to rights as soon as possible.' Gerald did as bid, and the grand total estimate came to a staggering £10500, the surveyor did not appear to be put out by the figure he had worked out, and made a quick call on his mobile to Mr Sinclair.

'Right Mr Parker, can you help me get the contact details of some local trades people, agricultural fencing specialists, landscape gardeners, joiners. I've got a tarmac contact for the pub car park so that can be sorted.' Gerald, spluttered surprised at such efficiency, 'Yes I'm sure I have contacts for all of them in my diary at home, I'll fetch them for you now. The surveyor then made a strange enquiry, 'And Mr Sinclair wants to know who owns the land where you set up your bird watching stations, was it no's 1/2/3/4 and 5. 'Why does he want to know that?' queried Gerald. 'Well,' responded the surveyor, 'When you have worked with Mr Sinclair as long as I have you learn not to ask questions, but be assured he'll have a good reason for it to be sure.' Gerald said, 'Okay but there may be different owners, Home Farm certainly has the sites Bill used for his north of village watch stations, but the church may own the bit behind the church which I think he said was station no 3. The other one on the other side of the river, where the gyrfalcon was seen hunting, I really don't know who that belongs to, but the other no 1 is definitely on Col James's land near the pub. 'Right then, here's my card can you let me have those land contacts as soon as possible, if you can get me those contractors details now I would appreciate it.' After the surveyor had left Gerald went see Bill and they wrote out the contact details of the various owners of the land that Bill had been given permission to site his bird watching stations on, and phoned them through to the surveyor.

The Contractors Descend on the Village

The next day the contractors arrived in the village, asking directions to Home Farm, the Stables, the Nature Reserve, and the Church. By early evening all of those areas had, had all the damage repaired with new fencing, damaged grass land was re-turfed and in some instances re-seeded, and finally they descended on the Crows Roost and began repairing all the fence and land damage behind the pub.

James and some of the locals were watching the contractors completing their work when the surveyor went up to James, 'Mr Fitzroy I need to know when we can be allowed to work on your car park.' 'What work on my car park?' he replied, 'I've only just sorted it, I had to get it done, all the gravel is evened out again now.' 'You don't understand Mr Fitzroy I need a clear 24 hours to get it completely resurfaced with tarmac,' cried the surveyor. 'But it wasn't tarmac, just gravelled,' pleaded James. 'Sorry but Mr Sinclair insists, your to get a newly surfaced car park, and some fancy gates, he says to keep out riff raff twitchers.' 'Oh well if he insists who am I to object,' cried James. 'Actually that's not all, Mr Sinclair wants to erect a proper bird Hide on your land where your Priory Bird Group put up their bird watching tent, station no 1 was it not, oh don't look like that, he'll pay the going rate if not more for the plot of land.' Col James Smith-Fitzroy stood back in amazement. The Rev Rosemary had come out from the bar, having heard part of the conversation. 'James don't you see Mr Sinclair clearly isn't about just repairing the damage his birders did, but about making amends, and leaving things much better than they were before he came.' James took on board what she was saying, 'Okay you can erect a Hide on my land, but consult with Mr Bill Taylor who leads the local birders about where to put it, since his lot will no doubt be using it mostly, and I guess it might attract a few a few normal bird watching types to come to my pub. 'Thanks, I'll get that sorted; just have to fix up a price with you, for the plot,' said the surveyor, 'Certainly not, no need to buy a plot the birders are welcome to have the use of the land down there, I might even have a go at this bird watching malarkey myself one day,' replied Col James.

'Excellent,' said the surveyor, 'Now I just have to visit these other land owners about putting Hides on their property, and who do I see about constructing a proper car park at your nature reserve?' Rosemary put in, 'I think that's the Lincolnshire Naturalists Association, but your going to see Bill aren't you he will definitely have a contact number for them.'

The Bird has Flown

The next morning after the invasion of the twitchers; Bill and Shelia Taylor and Sidney

Harding decided to check out all the watching stations. In the confusion of yesterdays events not all the tents had been disassembled or all the personal items of the watchers removed, and Bill was concerned that one specific pair of binoculars was missing. As they drove from station to station in the mini-bus, they collected several rucksacks, the missing binoculars, and two tents, along with other items. Whilst doing this they were all scanning the fens and the sea, in the hope of seeing another sighting of the falcon.

The saddened trio returned to Bill and Shelia's bungalow with the knowledge that the bird may have been scared away for good. As they supped their coffee the phone rang, 'Hi Bill its Rob at Blacktoft RSPB Reserve, on the Humber. I hear you might have seen an Icelandic Gyrfalcon down there?' Bill said, 'Yes but we think its been scared off, we got invaded by a large group of twitchers yesterday, its been havoc down here.' 'Oh dear, sorry to hear about that but every cloud has a silver lining, the birds just been seen up here again.' Rob went on to explain that one of the wardens had sighted an Icelandic gyrfalcon on Reads Island a couple of weeks ago but then it vanished, so the assumption is that the bird Bills group had seen was the same bird and it has now returned to the Humber.

As Bills group talked things through, they concluded that despite everything the Priory Bird Group had done well, and in reality the credit really had to go to young Geoffrey Thompson who first spotted the bird whilst bird watching on the

Reserve. What really had pleased them was the Twitcher Sinclair chap wanting to build some Hides for them. Bill had been asked to meet the surveyor and visit the sites with him, accompanied by the relevant landowners.

In due course with landowners consents, and a little money changing hands the Hides were erected, and by common agreement Hide No 2 was now called:

'Geoffrey's View'

Mr Sinclair refused an invitation to the official opening of the Hides organised by the Priory Birders, but he sent a nice letter explaining that he had been very pleased to pay the expenses of the project as recompense for his stupidity, but he certainly did not deserve to be thanked for his work, he said he would drop by some time to see them when passing, and wished them well for the future. Bill responded with a kindly response, making it clear that bygones were bygones, and if any rarities turned up again he promised to let him know providing he promised not to tell his friends

Chapter 8

The Riding School gets a new Owner

The Stables; which were formerly a part of Home Farm when it was owned by the Slater family had been run by old John Merrick since Mr Slater's death. He had brought it up cheaply from Mrs Slater when she sold most of Home Farm to his cousin Cyril Merrick. John had bought a few motley ponies and thought he would make a lot of money, by hiring them out to children over the summer holidays, but things had not worked out very well, and he was losing money and cutting corners. He had no insurance, and a year or so ago a young holiday maker had fallen off one of his ponies, because a strap on the saddle came away, due to lack of care of his old tack. A compensation claim had almost bankrupted him and he was forced to put the stables up for sale, but he was having great difficulty finding a buyer because of the state it was in.

'Well Mr Merrick this place is in a bit of a state isn't it,' declared a tall distinguished gentleman as he perused the yard, with piles of horse manure everywhere, stable doors hanging off their hinges and a dirty drinking trough in the centre of the yard. 'I suppose you could say that Mr Appleyard, but I do my best, getting too old for this sort of work now, but it's a good business you know,' responded a downcast John Merrick. 'Tell you what Mr Merrick I'll give you £100,000 for it cash no discussion, but I want it now, and you can vacate your old mobile home or take it with you somewhere else by the end of the week. John knew it was worth a lot more than that with its two paddocks, and access for pony trekking across the fens on permissive pathways and bridleways, but he was in no position to haggle. John wasn't worried about where he was going to live, because his cousin had said he could move his mobile home to a field adjacent to the stables, which was Home Farm property, in exchange for a few hours labouring on the farm every week.

Mr Appleyard was the local car dealer in the nearby seaside town of Reedsthorpe. He was sitting down to dinner at his large Edwardian Town House on the outskirts of the town, that evening with his wife Mavis and their only daughter twenty five year old Jolene. Jolene as the only daughter had led a pampered life; she was constantly partying with her former public school friends, the only work she had ever done was a bit of part time work in the reception of her Dads Garage. Her only real passion was horse riding, she had a horse called Fabian which she kept at a local livery stable just a few miles inland from Reedsthorpe.

Mr Appleyard addressed his daughter over the dinner table, 'Right Jolene your days of the high life are over, its time you settled down to doing a proper job, since you don't want to work in the business I've got something your mother and I think will keep you gainfully employed for years to come.' Jolene protested; 'But Dad, I haven't got time for a job, I have to keep up with my friends and there's Fabian to look after, and he's a full time job on his own.' Mrs Appleyard looked over to her husband and said, 'Come on Andrew lets go for a run over to Melton-Uppbury, we could pop in the Crows Roost for a drink and explain to Jolene what we have in mind.' So Andrew and Mavis Appleyard with their wary and reluctant daughter; drove off towards the village of Melton-Uppbury. 'Dad you've just passed the pub, what are you doing,' cried out Jolene as the car whizzed passed the Crows Roost Inn.

The Appleyards car pulled into the yard of a run down stables. Jolene pointed out a broken sign; ***Merricks Stables,*** which was hanging half upside down on the end of a wall. 'What are we doing in this dump Dad?' 'If you think I am working here you can think again, it's a dump.' She stamped her feet on the ground in a temper tantrum, one of the many her parents had seen over the years when Jolene did not get her own way. Her parents insisted on taking her on a tour of the yard, peeking in the tack room, and wandering around the paddocks. Stroppy Jolene continued protesting and pointed at John Merrick's derelict mobile home, 'What's that, you can't possibly expect me to work here and live in that thing.' Luckily John Merrick was over at Home Farm telling his cousin about the sale, he would have been quite upset about her disparaging comments about his home if he had heard them.

Jolene's parents waited until they were settled in a corner of the Crows Roost to give her the news. Andrew handed his daughter a sheaf of papers. She looked at them: ***Deeds and Title to Home Farm***

Stables known latterly as Merricks Stables: Agreement of Sale between John Merrick and Andrew Appleyard. 'You haven't really brought that run down place have you Dad?' 'Well yes I have, it's for you, you stupid girl, not much use to me is it.' Jolene joyfully cried out, 'Mine, you mean it's really for me, my own stables.' Andrew went on to explain how her mother and he had been looking round for months, to find a little business she might just enjoy running, when he heard about the sale of the stables from his friend Gerald Parker who had the General Store in Reedsthorpe. He then said, 'Have another look at the paperwork I just gave you, I've drawn up a few plans to see how we can best bring the place up to scratch, and tomorrow we are going to the council offices to see what permissions and licences we need for you to set it up as a proper riding school.' Mrs Appleyard chipped in, 'And of course Fabian will be getting a new home, his livery has cost us a bit over the years so at least your hobby might just cover his costs, and give you your own income at long last.'

Jolene realised the enormity of the task she was being given, but at the same time overjoyed. Having her own stables was a dream come true, her parents had never shown any interest in her horsey interests, and they certainly weren't too fussy on some of her former pony club friends. 'Too posh by half, they are, lazy idle rich kids, never done a days work in their lives, and your becoming like them you are,' those words of her Dads rattled round her head. Well she thought to herself, this was a turning point in her life. She intended to make this project a success. Not just for the sake of her parents, but also to show her friends that she was not just a party girl but could be an astute businesswoman as well.

'I think I should live at the stables when we get going,' she said to her parents. 'Well actually we are ahead of you my friend James Sotherby is looking at the possibility of importing one of those wooden Chalet type homes that can be erected in a couple of weeks or so, what do you think.' 'Sounds good to me dad,' cried Jolene, thinking not just my own business but freedom at last.

Chapter 9

The Village Remembers its Fallen Heroes

Gerald Parker was chairing the Parish Council Meeting in the village Hall by the Green. Kate Weatherspoon co-owner of the village shop was the Committees clerk, and Mrs Bottomly and Mrs Alderton long standing Parish Council members, new to the group was Col James Smith-Fitzroy owner and landlord of the Crows Roost Inn. He had decided to offer to go on the council, since he had taken on the role of local church benefactor as his ancestors had been. He was well aware that the Village Parish Council and the St Guthlac's Church Council were very closely linked, and what affected one invariably affected the other.

Col James had often sat in on Parish Council meetings but was never an elected member as such, but his previous interest in attending was to ensure his business was not going to be affected by any parish council decisions.

'Well it only remains for me to propose Col Smith-Fitzroy for election as a new member of our council, there being no other nominations, are there any objections to James joining us?' asked Gerald of the sitting members. All hands raised in approval of this popular man. The hall doors suddenly opened and in rushed the Rev Rosemary Fitter Rector of St Guthlac's, 'Sorry I'm late had to visit Jake Purdy, he's not too well, but still he can't half talk.' Rosemary was not a Parish Councillor but had an open invitation to observe, and make a contribution to the committee discussions, but not vote. She was keen to see James in reality her benefactor, more involved in village and church affairs, he had for reasons best known to himself kept himself out of such affairs for years just concentrating on running his pub since getting an early retirement from the army.

Rosemary had a soft spot for James and secretly hoped that one day he might acknowledge her as a women and not just a Priest; that he in effect paid the salary of. James was well known as a ladies man, he chatted all the women up, even sometimes Rosemary, but never when she had her clerical collar on, when possible she had taken to taking it off if she knew she was to be in this presence, but that opportunity did not occur too often.

'What about the War!' said Mrs Slater. Gerald responded, 'What do you mean Mrs Slater?' 'It's D Day on the 6th of June can't we do something in the village to remember those from here who died in the wars, Reedsthorpe Town Council are having a big two day event.' 'But we are only a little village Mrs Slater, we can't put on events like that can we Gerald?' protested Mrs Bottomly looking at Gerald.

James made his first mini speech to the committee, 'Do you know, Mrs Slater that was on my mind as well, you lost your older brother didn't you, in the last one.' 'Yes Thomas, he was only nineteen, Dad and Mum never could face up to his death, they pretended he was coming back any day for years until his name went up on the Reedsthorpe War Memorial.' 'Well I think the village should have an event to both commemorate our losses and celebrate the end of that awful period. I believe I can use a few contacts to call in a few favours. My former batman runs a Second World War re-enactment society, they are covering the Reedsthorpe event, but I'm sure they could include a parade through our village as a part of their programme.' Gerald realised he was losing control of the meeting, and they had veered off the agenda which involved planning consents and some financial matters. 'Thank you Councillor Smith-Fitzroy, we have a full agenda to get through yet, so I suggest we slot that possible suggestion into *Any Other Business,* would you see to that please Mrs Weatherspoon. Accordingly Kate marked *War Event* into the Any Other Business Slot, to be discussed just before the main meeting was completed.

Later that evening the proposals of Mrs Slater supported by James and the Rev Rosemary was accepted and Gerald arranged for another meeting to be held in the hall next week after James had spoken to his former Batman, and a few other x army friends. Mrs Slater suggested a land army theme as well, as a girl she remembered lots of land army girls working on her families farm, and a few scandals too involving some American airmen who been based at RAF Waddington, but were on temporary placement on the old private aerodrome near Reedsthorpe.

Enid was out walking her dog by the entrance to the village's bungalow cul-de-sac as Mrs Bottomly was heading out to the village shop. 'Oh good morning Edith,' Mrs Bottomly shouted out. 'And a very good morning to you Mrs Bottomly, I don't seem to have seen you about for a while,' she said. 'Actually your just the person I wanted to see,' said Mrs Bottomly.

'The Parish Council are wanting to hold a War Memorial Day in the village shortly.' 'But there's a big event on that theme taking place in Reedsthorpe,' explained Mrs Barrhead. 'Oh we know that, but Mrs Slater is really keen to commemorate the work of the land army girls, and Col Smith-Fitzroy is trying to arrange for a parade through the village of the second world war re-enactment society, they have a lot of old jeeps, ambulances and even a tank, apparently they will be at the Reedsthorpe event, but he says he should be able to get them to include our village on their days schedule since Reedsthorpe is so close, and their organiser is an old army friend of his.'

'Well what does that have to do with me?' queried Edith. 'That's easy you see we all remembered you once put on a display of old war time photos at the library, in fact it was quite a time ago,' Mrs Bottomly told her. 'Oh yes I did, didn't I but that was a lot of years ago, in fact I think it was in the early seventies, because I remember Harry and Kate from the shop were doing a school project at the time, so I got them to help me.' 'Gosh, so Harry and Kate went to school together, and must have become sweethearts then,' said Mrs Bottomly. 'Yes it was very sweet, and after all those years they are still together, and what a credit young Sophie is to them both,' replied Edith. 'So you see Mrs Barrhead what the committee wondered was if you could do something like it again, and get the library open for the weekend so everyone can see what it was really like here in those days.' 'But I retired a few years ago as you know, and it would have to be done by the present librarian not me.'

Mrs Bottomly stalled her by saying, 'Actually that's alright, I've spoken to Brenda at the library, and she says she hasn't got a clue about such things, but if you would like to go in and sort it out, she'll give you all the help she can, she said she would see about getting permission to open up on the Sunday, and the Saturday afternoon.'

Melton-Uppbury Village Library

Well I suppose it will keep me busy for a while, but what about Truffles, dogs are not allowed in the library are they, unless the rules have changed recently. 'We thought about that too, Brenda knew you had to tie Truffles up to the bike railings, when you collected books and how upset you get about it. So she said he could stay in the staff room while you worked on the project since it's was only her now working at the library, apart from her occasional holiday relief, from the Reedsthorpe Branch.

Edith's Project Working Area in the Village Library

Edith Barrhead after a little thought agreed to undertake the task, in fact she felt it would be quite exciting almost like going back to work, but without pay. Not that Enid was short of money having worked all her working life for the Library Service she had a vey good pension, and a pretty big widows pension from the bank her late husband worked at.

Mrs Bottomly reported back to the other committee members that Mrs Barrhead aided by Brenda would set up a display of wartime photographs and documents for the set weekend. Jack Wilkinson was contacted and he agreed to get some of his museums wartime collection, and bring it along to be set up in the village hall or library which ever suited best. So the weekend war event began to take shape, with locals pitching in to help where they could.

Alf Pritchard was talking to Dr Clutterbuck in the Crows Roost Inn about arranging the next meeting of the Historical Group when, when they were interrupted by Gerald Parker, 'Nigel, Alf I guess you have heard about our plan to hold a war weekend in the village to coincide with the events running in Reedsthorpe.' 'Yes of course, all the old timers are quite excited about it I hear,' said Nigel. 'Well that's it you see, I thought really that since we are all involved with the historical group we should put something on ourselves,' Gerald said. 'But we set ourselves up to research the past history of the area, not more recent events,' protested Nigel, 'Anyway we don't have any research material or artefacts from the wars.' Alf piped up, 'Yes we do, I have.'

Alf's Unique War Collection Revealed

'Tell you what come round to my house and I'll show you, you might be quite surprised. The trio drank up their pints and walked round to the council estate where Alf lived. He led them down the side of his house to a large shed at the bottom of a long path, the garden was overgrown, and they had to use their hands to brush aside the overgrown branches of shrubs and trees. They faced a locked door, Alf had a multitude of locks and chains on the door, and the only window was shuttered. 'God Alf its like Fort Knox,' exclaimed Gerald. As Alf opened each of the locks he turned to the two men and said, 'What ever you do don't touch anything some of these things might be live.' They entered the darkened shed and tried to adjust their eyes to the darkness until Alf located a large battery lamp, which had an intensely powerful and wide beam. They stood back aghast; the whole of the shed was stacked up with mainly Second World War military ware, shells of all shapes and sizes, bullets and magazines of shells. Several hand guns that you normally see on films about life in the first war trenches. A couple of Lee Enfield rifles, uniforms and helmets. A clean hardly worn Civil Defence Uniform carefully folded in a plastic protector hanging on a hook at the far end of the shed. 'That was my dads, but not from the war from the nineteen sixties the cold war, which no one seems to talk about any more.'

'My, My, young Alf you're a dark horse, we never knew you had all this did we Nigel,' gasped Gerald looking over to Nigel. Alf then produced a large loose leafed folder, and said, 'Every single item is in here, with an entry telling a bit about where each item came from. Look he pointed to an entry:

20th November 1954 (1 X Government Issue Gas Mask) from Gran Lizzie.
30th October 1954 (2 pairs 10 x50 Army Issue Field glasses) from Reedsthorpe army and navy store.

They were both amazed, this was a unique collection; it transpired that Alf's Dad had started the collection shortly after the war, and when he died a few years ago Alf took it over, he felt close to his Dad when he was alone in the shed reading some of his Dads notes, and handling the items his Dad had so carefully preserved. He remembered what a privilege it felt when his Dad sat him on his knee in the shed and tried to explain to an eight year old what the shells were used for, or why we had to have gas masks, and build Anderson shelters in our gardens. Alf had added quite a lot to the collection with his metal detecting of known military installations locally, but some of these items were of concern; because the army bomb squad had, not examined some of the shells.

Gerald asked Alf why he kept it all hidden away, and Alf's response was that he did it to preserve his Dads memory. Nigel eventually persuaded Alf to show Jack Wilkinson his collection, with a view to possibly putting on a permanent exhibition at the Reedsthorpe Museum with a dedication to his Dad who served as a gunner on HMS Troutbridge in 1943-5.

The Village War Day

June the 6th came upon them too soon in reality, to do the War Day in Melton-Uppbury any real justice it had needed to be planned at least a year beforehand not in two or three weeks as it was in this case. But by pulling together all was prepared in time.

A short memorial service was conducted in the hall. Col James's army friends turned trumps. Their re-enactment society not only did the one planned parade through the village and round the green on their way through to Reedsthorpe, with their mainly second world war ambulances, jeeps and tank and uniformed personnel, but they came back that evening and did it again. This time stopping to join the villagers hospitality, the non-drivers taking full advantage to Col James's bar in the village hall.

Elderly Mrs Alderton whispered in Mrs Bottomly's ear, 'All these lovely young men in uniform it does bring back memories of when I was a teenager,' she blushed and rushed off home as if she had let slip a dreadful secret. Mrs Bottomly let her imagination go as she thought about what Mrs Alderton had just said, but was disturbed when a huge crash occurred in the hall, a display stand had been pushed over and a young man in uniform was splayed out across it on his back, having just received a punch on the chin from young Geoffrey Thompson. Sophie Weatherspoon who was dressed up as a land army girl was trying to restrain Geoffrey as he tried to continue his assault on the young pretend soldier. 'It was only a kiss, it didn't mean anything, he was only trying to be friendly,' protested Sophie. But Geoffrey had earlier overheard the said young man talking on the green to one of his mates, betting each other, who would get off with a certain girl before the night was out, not knowing that the girl in question was his sometimes girlfriend Sophie, until he saw both the lads eyeing Sophie up in the hall, a few minutes ago.

Col James came over and grabbed the lad in uniform, by the collar and ejected him from the hall, but not knowing the full story, also ejected Geoffrey. Mrs Bottomly looked on, thinking to herself, 'Yes as Mrs Alderton said its brings back memories of the old days.'

Enid put on a really excellent display of old war time photos and documents in the library, luckily most of the stuff she had used previously for the school children a good few years ago was still stored away exactly where she had left it in the library loft. 'Oh how time has stood still, but my how I have aged in the process,' thought Enid.

Alf Pritchard had got together with Jack from the Reedsthorpe Museum to go through his Dads collection of war memorabilia. Between them they managed to set up a unique display of armoury and associated war artefacts in the village hall. This proved to be of great interest to the former army friends of James Smith-Fitzroy. Alf found himself inundated with requests from the members of the re-enactment society to buy various bits of his collection. He agreed to sell a lot of the pieces he himself had collected, but none that was collected by his Dad.

Alf had been persuaded, at the suggestion of Nigel and Gerald to give most of it, minus a few very select personal bits of his Dads to the Reedsthorpe Museum. Jack was to set up a memorial plaque to Alf's Dad, and publicly acknowledge that Alf had donated it to the museum. Alf was really chuffed to think that hundreds of people over the next few years would see the collection, with his name as the donor affixed to the glass cases, and his Dads war record proudly displayed along with his medals. To really seal the deal Jack had announced that in a few months time when he and his volunteers had sorted through all the stuff Alf had given them, and bought new display cabinets and display stands on which to display them, he was going to organise an exhibition opening, with Alf Prichard as the special VIP guest. The Melton-Uppbury Historical Group and the museum volunteers would have an evening of celebration, wine and cheese, if not more in the museum.

Trip to Flag Fen

It was Saturday the 10th of July as the Reedsthorpe Mini Bus Taxi pulled into the Rectory Drive. Members of the Melton-Uppbury Historical Group stood about waiting for Nigel Clutterbuck to come out of his house. Gerald Parker as Chairman of the Group took charge and, ticked off the names of each person as they climbed onto the bus. Eventually Nigel come out being fussed by his wife Julie, she saw him onto the bus and passed him his packed lunch, as she did so she yelled up to everyone, 'Sorry folks I can't come I've got a drama club rehearsal today, last minute nerves of our Director for next's weeks performance,' looking over to Gerald she added, 'Gerald would you mind keeping an eye on Nigel he had a bit of a turn last night but insists on coming, you know what he's like.' Gerald leaned out of the bus and said, 'Don't worry we'll watch out for him.' The Driver turned to Gerald and said, 'So where are we off to mate, told its Peterborough is that right?' Nigel having settled himself in one of the front seats said, 'Here I've worked out a route, we are going to a place called Flag fen it's a prehistoric site open air museum near Peterborough, but if you follow the route I've planned we can avoid the city.' The driver cheerfully took the map from Nigel, 'Right lets have a look then, as he perused the map and Nigel's suggested route plan.'

Down to Reedsthorpe on the A52, down to Boston and onto the A16 bypassing Spalding, then turning southeast on the A1073 through Crowland down to the A47 eastwards turning south on the B1040 to the village of Whittlesey.

'Right then, that looks good, avoiding Peterborough is a good idea, its chaos there on a Saturday anyway, everyone on board who should be,' he yelled out. Everyone cheered, as the bus drove out into Church Lane with Julie Clutterbuck waving them all off.

Gerald whispered in Sophie's ear, 'Right Sophie could you be a darling and collect everyone's dues.' He then addressed the bus passengers, 'Right all of you, Sophie's coming round in a few minutes to collect the fare and museum entrance fees, as you will remember it was to be £8 per person.' Sophie soon collected up the dues from the group members. On the trip were, Alf Pritchard, Silas

Pestell, Enid Barrhead, Jack Wilkinson, Rosemary Fitter, Sidney Harding, and Dorothy Burton from Lincoln, not a group member but invited by her friend Rosemary. Sophie had invited Geoffrey but he was out for the day with the Priory Birders. Sophie's dad was a group member but couldn't come having the shop to look after, which she was very pleased about, Pity Geoffrey wasn't here though,' she thought to herself.

Nigel counted up the money 10x£8=£80 and gave the driver £50 keeping the rest for their reduced rate group entry fees.

An hour and a half later the bus pulled into the car park of the Flag Fen Archaeology Park on Northey Road. They were all disembarking from the bus when Nigel saw Francis Prior the Site Director getting into his car. Nigel called out to the others and they watched Francis of the famous Time Team Programmes drive out, he waved at them. Sophie said to Alf, 'I can't believe it, that's two famous people we have seen from the television recently.' 'Who's the other one,' he replied. 'Charlie Dimmock of course, at the fete last year,' said Sophie. 'Oh I didn't know her, I'm not interested in gardens,' he replied. 'Nor was I, but its good to see television people, they are after all no different to us,' said Sophie. Alf responded, 'Oh yes they are, they are bloody rich.'

The group went into the visitor centre, and all opted to go into the café before walking through the park. In the meantime Nigel and Gerald went over to the reception desk to pay the entrance fees. 'Right Sir that's ten times three pounds which is just thirty pounds please, ' said the lady at the desk. 'Have you been before?' she asked. 'No its our first time here,' replied Gerald. 'Right then you will need these,' as she counted out ten leaflets containing a map of the site. 'We have people all over the site if you have any questions, and the toilets are clearly marked.'

After a quick cup of tea Gerald gathered up the group and distributed the maps. 'Its all clearly mapped out so we don't need to stay in a group, just split up as you like, but lets meet up at the round houses in about three quarters of an hour.'

Nigel's Photo of a Round House

As they walked along the pathway they passed several small paddocks containing Soay Sheep, which were apparently a very ancient breed, which would have been domesticated by Bronze Age people. They passed by a lake to a large building which contained the preserved remains of a prehistoric wooden walk way. It was a huge building with a raised walkway all around it, and interpretation boards, explaining in detail exactly what they were looking at. The preserved remains were dark brown and glistened, because there was a constant water sprinkling system wetting them. Sophie was the last to leave the building and got talking to one of the volunteer staff; who took her to see a replica dug out canoe that was tied up to a post in the lakes reed bed next to the walkway building. He told Sophie she could have a go in it if she liked, she sat in it but felt it was very unstable and declined the offer of a paddle.

At the replica round houses Dr Clutterbuck was describing to the group how bronze age man lived over 3000 years ago. Sophie caught up with Alf who was standing at the back of a crowd of people outside of one of the round houses. She could hear Dr Clutterbuck talking at the front. It appears that when Nigel was talking to his group lots of other visitors joined up, thinking he was an official guide. An elderly lady joined them at the back of the crowd with a badge on her coat saying, [**FLAG FEN VISITOR GUIDE**] she whispered to Alf, 'He's very good isn't he, must be a new volunteer, I haven't seen him before, certainly knows more than I do.' Sophie and Alf looked at each other and smiled.

After a while the crowd dispersed, and a flustered Nigel, asked, 'Who were all those people, one minute I was talking to Silas and Enid, next thing it was all strangers and that American couple asking all those awkward questions.' 'Come on Nigel your moment of fame as a famous Professor is over, its time to head back,' said Gerald taking Nigel by the arm. Back at the visitor centre they had time to look in at the Roman Herb Garden, and buy a few bits and pieces from the shop. Nigel brought Sophie a guidebook to Flag Fen, and also a County Guidebook to the Pre-Reformation Monastic Sites of Lincolnshire.

On the bus home as they were driving up the B1040, Sophie saw a sign for Crowland Abbey, she went up to the front of the bus and showed Dr Clutterbuck the page in her Monastic Site Guide Book that referred to Crowland Abbey. 'Could we stop off and see the abbey since we have to pass it anyway,' she pleaded. Nigel said to Gerald, 'What do you think, have we got time?' Gerald leaned forward to the driver who was listening in to the conversation. 'No problem mate, but can you make sure we only spend half an hour there, I promised the Mrs we could out on the town tonight,' replied the driver. 'Good we'll do that I'm sure most people will appreciate seeing another site of interest anyway,' said Gerald. Sophie went back telling the rest of the group what they were up to. The minibus trundled up a narrow lane towards the Abbey, and parked in one of the two car parks.

The group disembarked for their short excursion, while Nigel, Gerald and Sophie walked round the substantial Abbey remains, Alf, Silas and Sidney Harding nipped down the lane to the pub. The others led by Rosemary, Jack, Enid and Dorothy went into the Abbey Church, which was still in daily use as the Parish Church and open to visitors.

Nigel's Photo of Crowland Abbey

The group were dropped back at the Rectory dead on 6 pm as planned. Gerald made a small collection for the driver to have a couple of pints, who then went on his way back to Reedsthorpe, to hit the town with his wife for a night out. Everyone meandered to their respective homes having all enjoyed the day, especially Alf, Silas and Sidney who had each managed to down a pint or two at the Crowland Village Oldie World Pub, and were now headed for the Crows Roost Inn for more. Gerald had been invited to have a nip or two at the Rectory with Nigel. Jack collected his car and headed back to his house in Reedsthorpe.

Chapter 10

Dorothy gets an indecent Proposal

Rosemary Fitter was packing her things in the clergy flat in Reedsthorpe. She had been supposed to vacate it three weeks ago, but she hadn't secured any new accommodation for herself and had just booked into a bed and breakfast guesthouse on the sea front in Reedsthorpe, as a temporary measure.

As she was packing she felt a touch of remorse at having thrown her lot in with St Guthlac's Church in Melton-Uppbury, for not only was she now homeless but also had agreed to accept a little less in remuneration from the local church council, than she had previously been getting from the diocese. Added to which the work load was so light now, that she was becoming very bored.

Friend of Rosemary, twenty five year old Dorothy Burton had now completed her third year of studies at the Lincoln Theological College. Her divorce from her husband had now been settled. She was awaiting the outcome of her examinations and had decided she wanted a few days holiday to collect her thoughts and think about the future. She thought she might stay with Rosemary for a while, but had forgotten that Rosemary was having a hell of a job house or flat hunting. She rang Rosemary for an update.

'Hi Dorothy I was just going to ring you, I'm just packing, most of my stuff is going to have to go in the store cupboard downstairs, I've had to book a B and B for a bit, high season prices as well,' poor Rosemary complained. 'Oh that's awful surely someone in the village can help?' suggested Dorothy. 'Well I've had an advert in Kate's shop window for ages now and not had a single response,' said Rosemary. 'Well haven't you asked James if he could help its practically his church now isn't it? Tell you what can you book me into your B and B for tonight and we can see James this afternoon and explore the possibilities, I'm sure he'll do what he can to help, I can be down there by half one if I leave now,' said Dorothy.

Trust Dorothy to be practical, Rosemary had not wanted to speak to James about her accommodation problem in case he thought she was suggesting she move in with him, which would answer all her personal problems of course, she still dreamed about the possibility of such happening. Unfortunately he had seemed to become less attracted to her than he seemed to be last year, it was only when she was in Dorothy's company that he flirted outrageously as was his want.

Dorothy's banger of a car spluttered to a halt outside number 103 The Parade in Reedsthorpe. Rosemary was waiting on the steps to welcome her. Rosemary had cleared her church flat, stored most of her possessions in the office store cupboard, and moved her essentials to her room in the guesthouse. Her room was a twin bedded room so Dorothy would be able to stay in her room, and since Rosemary was paying the going double room price anyway, it would not cost Dorothy anything.

The girls tidied up the room and left the guesthouse and headed for Melton-Uppbury in Rosemary's slightly more reliable transport. As they travelled the ten to fifteen minute drive

Rosemary, bemoaned her decision to take up the full time post at St Guthlac's. 'But Rosemary why did you take up the offer in the first place?' 'Because I thought James fancied me, I think, and I thought he might just ask me to marry him and move into the pub flat, I thought that was why he asked me to take up the Rectors post,' replied Rosemary. 'But surely you know he flirts with every woman of every age, he even chats up young Sophie and old Mrs Barrhead, and don't you remember how he was with my friend Charlie last year?' 'I know I've been stupid, you might be young Dorothy but you have at least been married, I'm in my thirties and only ever had one sort of a relationship and that was a disaster,' replied a sorry for her self, Rosemary.

They parked up at the church, something they had both done almost every time they were going to the Crows Roost Inn, not a good idea to advertise the fact that the local female priest liked a tipple or two. It was only a short walk down church lane back to the main road and down to the pub.

They looked an odd couple, Rosemary being a little overweight, wearing a dark long dress and horn rimmed glasses, frumpish some might say, but she was only in her mid thirties. Dorothy on the other hand looked as unlike a theology student as one could get. Slim with short black hair, tight denim jeans and a short black, leather bikers jacket and a small pixyish attractive face, some might say gothic looking, and of course a good ten years younger than Rosemary.

As they passed the Rectory gates, they saw Julie Clutterbuck weeding the drive. 'Afternoon Julie you look busy,' yelled out a cheery Dorothy. Rosemary was in a bit of a daze and had been for the millionth time comparing herself to her little best friend Dorothy, and thinking about the little ironies that life presented to each of us. Some of us had it and others didn't. Certainly she felt, no she knew Dorothy had it, and she didn't.

'Come on wake up Rosemary', cried out Dorothy. Julie said, 'Is Rosemary alright?' 'Yes she's fine just worried.' 'What are you worried about?' asked Julie. Rosemary caught on and said, 'Just where I'm going to live, had to vacate the flat this morning, and had to move into a guest house.'
Julie looked in deep thought for a moment and said, 'God I thought it was something serious dear, look let me have a word with Nigel this evening, best to catch him when he's on the whisky, I've an idea.'

Col James Smith-Fitzroy was behind the bar talking to Len the church sexton, when the girls came into the pub. James looked up with a huge welcoming smile on his face, 'What can I get for my favourite two young women?' Dorothy quick as a flash replied, 'Less of the flattery James, we both know you have the hots for that nurse Felicity Oundle of the Priory Birders Group.' He laughed and served them their respective drinks, and they went over to a small table near the window. 'I must go to the little girls room,' Dorothy said to Rosemary, 'I knew I should have gone at your place.'

Len and James got back to their topic for the day, the threat posed to the UK by terrorists. Dorothy walked the length of the bar to the ladies at the other end of the pub. James stopped talking as his eyes followed her trim figure, tight jeans, and tight little jacket. Len caught his eye and said, 'You can forget that, she's but a young lass, but by God she does have a fantastic carriage, and any way you know Rosemary's much more your type.' 'One can but dream,' replied James as he watched Dorothy vanish from view. James pondered on Lens revelation, yes perhaps Rosemary was more his type, nearer his age a tad he being fifty-five years young, even Rosemary was too young for him in reality. When Dorothy returned both Len and James couldn't help allowing their eyes to follow her slow progress, was she doing it on purpose, they were both thinking.

'Dorothy did you know James and Len were lusting after you just then?' 'Of course I did silly, why do you think I took my time,' replied a smiling Dorothy. 'Wish I could get half as much attention,' moaned Rosemary. 'Its being a vicar that puts men off Rosemary not you as a person,' replied a supportive Dorothy. 'Look have you forgotten what we came here for, in fact why I came over from Lincoln for?' said Dorothy. 'Oh yes I suppose accommodation, but I can't ask James now can I?' cried Rosemary, 'He's only got eyes for you.' 'No perhaps not, but I can, leave it with me,' said Dorothy as she stood up and very slowly walked over to the bar.

James and Len looked up as Dorothy came to the bar. 'Right young lady same again.' 'No not yet I wondered if I might have a quiet chat, if you can spare me a few minutes. James face lit up as he followed Dorothy out of earshot of Rosemary and

Len. Len muttered under his breath, 'The old buggers still got it dirty git.'

'Well what can I do for you,' he politely asked. 'Actually I'm looking for accommodation,' she replied. 'What kind of accommodation, house bungalow flat,' he said. 'Well anything really, even flat share but its got to be in Melton.' 'Have you finished your theology degree at Lincoln?' 'Oh yes just waiting for the results. James looked into those beautiful eyes of Dorothy's and placed his hand on her knee and said, 'I think I have a proposal that might just suit everyone.' 'What's that then?' she said as she gently lifted his hand off her knee. 'Well my flats far too big for one, so I suppose I could let out one of my spare bedrooms.' 'What about if your tenant wanted to have friend stay over,' she said thinking of herself. 'That's okay I always have a guest bedroom ready, not that it gets much use these days.' Dorothy responded, 'Sounds great to me, but wouldn't the villagers talk a bit if they knew you were sharing your flat with a younger woman.' 'Who cares, let them talk any way perhaps my tenant might want a bit more than just a room, I said I'd never get married but under the circumstances I could be easily tempted, and my wife would became a very rich woman with my inheritance from the hoard you found last year.'

As Dorothy and James walked back to the bar, James invited Dorothy to view the flat. She called over to Rosemary, 'Come on we are going to have a look at James bedrooms. The three of them went up the stairs, James insisting that Rosemary led the way, he followed very closely behind Dorothy he could almost smell her. His imagination went into overdrive thinking of the possibility of Dorothy living with him, but he awoke to reality when he heard Rosemary shouting down, 'Are you two coming or what?' Dorothy had by now realised that James was offering her a room not Rosemary, so she had slowly climbed the stairs trying to work out how to handle it. Unbelievably as she climbed the stairs she could feel the strong sexual vibes coming from James, and in fact it had turned her on. As they entered the flat she had to sit down for a moment to recompose her self.

James tried to cover up his naughty thoughts, but when he looked at Dorothy he knew that she knew what he knew and yet she was still smiling. Dorothy sprung into evasive action; she couldn't let her friend down after all, could she, even though she too would shortly be looking for somewhere to live. Well which room would it be,' said Dorothy innocently. 'That one at the end of the hall,' as he pointed it out Rosemary charged along the hall, and pushed the door open. It was a big airy room, with large windows looking over the pub car park; it had a sink and built in wardrobes. James and Dorothy entered the room as Rosemary was bouncing on the bed, how strange thought James still being none the wiser. 'Afraid you'd have to share the bathroom,' said James looking directly into Dorothy's eyes, 'But I don't mind you leaving your undies all over the place, I wont mind tidying them up.' Dorothy had really accidently set James up for a huge fall. It would be more than his pride she'd be hurting, but the thought of him finding Rosemary's smalls all over his flat instead of hers was too much, she liked him and this was cruel although very much unintentional. This could hurt both of them she had to take action, 'Come on Rosemary, quick we have something to do urgently it can't wait.' She ushered Rosemary down the stairs and straight out to the car, she stopped for a second and yelled up to James who was still standing at the top of the stairs.

'Give it a couple of weeks and I'll let you know, thanks anyway.' James stood at the top of the stairs for a while trying to fathom out exactly what had just happened, when Len shouted up the stairs, 'Get your arse down here soldier boy, leave those girls be and serve your bloody customers.' Len had been quietly topping up his drink anyway and hadn't noticed that Rosemary and Dorothy had already left. 'What bloody customers Len?' 'Me of course,' retorted Len. 'But you've hardly supped your pint since I last filled it,' cried James. 'Well I couldn't have you taking advantage of that young Dorothy could I, after all I have church responsibilities and she might be a vicar one day,' said Len slyly winking at poor old James, who was by now thinking he had gone too far 'marriage indeed'.

James slowly came to realise how silly he had been, he got knackered just taking Enid's dog for a walk, how could he keep up in bed with a young filly like Dorothy. What he did not know was what the young filly herself was really thinking. As Rosemary and Dorothy were walking back to the church passing the Rectory, Nigel was just coming out to walk up to the shop.

'Hi girls, Julie has just been telling me about you needing somewhere to live, Rosemary why don't you pop round the front and see her, she's at that top flower bed again. 'Okay, thanks Nigel we will,' said Dorothy hurrying Rosemary in front of her. 'Oh glad you called back, didn't have to wait for Nigel to get in a good mood he was telling me he had seen a Ad in the shop yesterday, someone looking for accommodation, he thought we might let the back bedroom out, help out with the upkeep of this old house. When I said it might be you he was pleased as punch, said a Rectory was the right place for the Rector to live, and next to the church as well.'

With that Julie took them into the house through the conservatory then through the kitchen to the hall, up the wide stairwell that circled to the next floor. Along a short corridor to an end bedroom, which was large with an old double bed, old-fashioned closet these days called en suites, and two large windows facing up to the Church and the Rookery. Dorothy spoke first, 'Well what do you think, Rosemary its ideal?' 'But what about?' blurted out Rosemary, thinking about James and the flat. Dorothy forestalled her from saying anymore saying, 'Forget that this is a better option.' 'Yes I do believe it is, but can I make a few improvements?' pleaded Rosemary. 'Of course you can dear, we can't afford to get it done up but if you want to improve things you'd be welcome to do so, there's a little room next door, that's it with a window, as you can see we don't use it for anything now, you could make it into a little kitchenette, you'd be welcome to use my kitchen but if you have visitors, other than those people like Dorothy who we know well we'd prefer them to stay up in your bit of the house, hope you don't mind.'

'That's fantastic,' cried out Rosemary, 'I'll get started on the place tomorrow if I can.' Dorothy said, 'I'll be able to help out, I've got plenty of time now having finished my course.'

As they walked up to the church, Rosemary said, 'At last I have something to celebrate, I've hated living on my own since you went back to college last year.' Last year Dorothy as a theology student spent three months living with Rosemary in Reedsthorpe, while she did research on St Guthlac's Church for her dissertation.

Rosemary then said, 'So lets not go back to the guest house yet, lets dine back at the Crows Roost to celebrate after all it was your idea to spend the afternoon finding me some where to live.' 'Okay then, I suppose I will have to limit my drinking while you get pissed again, so I can get us back to Reedsthorpe,' protested Dorothy, thinking of how she would be able to get out of the mix up with James. She thought about him behind her on the stairs again, and felt flushed, could she possibly resist him if he really tried it on, it was nearly two years since she last did anything with her x husband, and had kept away from men since then, not for any particular reason other than wanting to get her theology course completed.

James was surprised when he saw Dorothy and Rosemary coming back into the bar, he wasn't sure what to say, best keep mum he thought, for the time being anyway. The bar was getting busy the early evening crowd were coming in, so he nudged Helen his barmaid to serve them while he thought things through and served some regulars.

Later that evening Rosemary was quite tipsy, they had both enjoyed a meal, Dorothy had a chicken curry, but Rosemary pigged out on a large cod and chips. Dorothy left Rosemary who was muttering to herself, to go to the ladies.

James was clearing a table when he saw her passing, he grabbed her arm gently and whispered, 'Look Dorothy I think I owe you a big apology.' She turned and faced him with those big eyes that melted his heart, 'No you don't James your just a man, I was married you know so I do know about basic instincts.' He looked relieved, and said, 'And about marriage and all that stuff, I'm sorry I was so excited I just started gabbling.' Dorothy replied sympathetically, 'That's all right but I doubt if I'll get married again, but about the room.' 'Yes the room tell you what, you can still have it if you want it no conditions.' Dorothy thought again about the possibility of giving in to temptation, 'No promises yet, I might get a job miles away after I graduate, but if I decide to stay about I might just take up your offer.' As she walked off to rejoin Rosemary, James couldn't take his eyes off her rear, Len sitting in his usual corner caught on and made up his mind to wind James up about it later on. Dorothy looked at her watch and realised it was pretty late, and she had to collect Rosemary's car from the church. She left Rosemary talking gibberish to a couple she didn't know and walked up the church. Ten minutes later Dorothy and James's were lifting Rosemary into the car, as they did so Rosemary flung her arms round James's neck and cried out, 'I love you James marry me.' James and Dorothy gave a sigh of relief as

Rosemary slipped into the passenger seat, and were pleased that there was no one about to witness the spectacle.

Dorothy couldn't resist giving James a peck on the cheek as she tried to bypass him getting into the car, they embraced tightly too tightly for a second or two, as she slid behind the wheel and drove off back to Reedsthorpe, knowing she might not be able to resist a second time. She felt like a traitor but lets face it she was a free agent and so was James, would Rosemary have felt guilty given similar circumstances she wondered.

The next morning Dorothy woke up in Rosemary's guesthouse room, she looked over to the other bed, the loud snoring had persisted for most of the night, and Dorothy had little sleep. The smell of stale booze pervaded the room even with all the windows open.

Dorothy went down for breakfast feeling guilty about James; she knew Rosemary would have a huge headache and certainly would be sick if she had breakfast so left her to sleep on. Luckily no one said anything over breakfast about the noise on the main stairs last night as Dorothy slowly dragged Rosemary to her bed. When Rosemary eventually surfaced, the unreality of her performance last night at the pub hit home. 'Am I moving in with James then?' she asked Dorothy. 'No have you forgotten, we are doing up that room in the Rectory you are going to live there.' 'Oh but didn't James give me a big smacker on the lips last night, after we looked at the room he said I could have,' cried out Rosemary.

'No he did not, it was you that grabbed him and gave him a big smacker, you were pissed don't you remember?' said Dorothy. 'Oh God did every one see me?' appealed a distraught Rosemary. 'Luckily not, but if you keep drinking like that you might just lose your job and all your friends, its not a very good portrayal of a typical female priest is it.' 'Oh God, its just that when I think about James and getting married I get carried away,' she cried. As Rosemary sobered up Dorothy explained about the mix up in James's flat, and explained that was why she rushed her out to save any embarrassment. That James was none the wiser, thank goodness. And how fortuitous it was when they met up with Julie and the offer of accommodation at the Rectory. Dorothy left out the bits concerning James and herself, and in the cold light of day thoughts of guilt washed away, after all nothing really had happened had it.

Later that next day Rosemary and Dorothy went to Reedsthorpe Market and spent ages looking for decorating bits and pieces, but couldn't find what they wanted. So they ended up at Mr Gerald Parkers General Store in Reedsthorpe; buying paint, brushes and a weird black wallpaper that Dorothy thought would look great on one of the walls. Rosemary however had her doubts, but allowed herself to be persuaded. The next few days saw them decorating and getting Rosemary's new room at the Rectory turned into a homely little bedsit. A local kitchen fitter was employed to convert the tiny room next to the bedroom into a kitchenette.

Reedsthorpe Open Market

A few days later Dorothy popped into the pub and came clean with James about the mix up, and why Rosemary had thought he had proposed to her, 'It was my fault entirely, I should have made it clear that I was looking for accommodation for Rosemary,' she said. 'I understand completely, and it explains why Rosemary did what she did,' he said sympathetically, 'But I am a bit worried about Rosemary's drinking, people are beginning to talk, after all she is now our church Rector.' Dorothy told James she had spoken to Rosemary about it, and it had been agreed that she would limit her drinking when out in public, if she wanted a proper drink she would have to do it at home. Dorothy continued, 'The trouble is Rosemary loves her job, but I think she is desperate to get settled in a relationship, I think she has thought for some time she and you might make a good match, and that's why she drinks a little too much, she's quite unhappy and instead of just having a social drink she sometimes drinks to forget her personal circumstances.'

Poor James was stumped for words, a relationship with Rosemary had never seriously entered his head, not even when Len suggested it in jest, he thought back to the many times he had flirted a bit with her, but it was always when Dorothy was present, and his attentions were always focused on her not Rosemary, any attention he had given to Rosemary had been really to divert attention from his real feelings. Even so it was a pipe dream, he knew there was no chance of twenty five year old Dorothy ever fancying an older man like himself, especially one so set in his ways, as he undoubtedly was, being a lifelong bachelor.

Dorothy went back to the Rectory to get on with decorating Rosemary's new room. A confused James scratched his head wondering exactly what was going on, would he ever fathom out the mind of a woman. Len yelled over from his corner near the bar, 'Come on Soldier Boy, stop thinking about young Dorothy and serve me a bloody pint.'

The Origins of the Fitzroy Treasure Hoard Solution

Enid Barrhead was in the village library collecting yet another *Agatha Raisein Murder Mystery* when she spotted Julie Clutterbuck sitting in the reference section corner, reading a book. Good Morning Julie are you well?' she said as she walked over to her. 'Oh! Enid you gave me quite a start there, yes I'm fine,' she said. 'Good book,' asked Enid. 'Well actually Enid, Nigel and I were talking the other day, and we were trying to figure out how there was so much treasure in that tomb. You see all the evidence from the literary sources, that you found out about if you remember last year, made it clear that the Saxon Priory was very poor, and the Norman Priory that followed on wasn't thought to be much better off, other wise as Nigel said Henry VIII would have ceased it, and given it to his fair weather friends.'

'So that's why you are reading up on, *The Treasure Hoards of Lincolnshire*,' said Enid, reading the title of the book Julie was studying. She continued, 'Actually most of it I believe was probably the Fitzroy's family property, hidden away in the priory for safe keeping.' Julie replied, 'But what about the coins, they were Pre-Norman, weren't they Anglo Saxon, and some were from all over Europe, if I remember correctly.' Enid said, 'Well I suppose the first Fitzroy's may have collected taxes from the local Saxons when they were first given lands by William the Conqueror, and although the dates of the coins don't match up perhaps the really old coins were the only ones in circulation at the time.' Julie said, 'I suppose that could explain it, I'll have a chat with Nigel tonight and let you know what he thinks.'

That evening Enid had just got in having taken Truffles for his last walk on the beach of the day when the phone rang. 'Hi Enid, its Julie, just had a chat about the coins with Nigel, he thinks you are right, he checked up and found that there were very few British coins minted in the period 800-1066, so that explains why there were so many old coins in circulation, he thinks the Fitzroy's may well have kept back some of the collected taxes for themselves, if they indeed collected them.' Enid replied, 'Thanks Julie, but if you hadn't been thinking about treasures I wouldn't have thought about it.' 'I suppose as Nigel says we might never really know the truth, but it's a logical conclusion to the problem, until such time as some new evidence emerges,' said Julie. They both settled down in their respective homes having possibly solved one of the major questions raised about the monastic treasure found last year, the treasures that saved their Parish Church.

A Find at the Rectory

Rosemary and Dorothy had cleared out the bedroom; Rosemary had decided to invest in some new furnishings for her room, a new bed, a desk, a dressing table, and a small sofa settee just in case she had a friend to stay over. Dorothy and Rosemary selected a suitable bed settee out of the Argos Catalogue and ordered it on line; Dorothy chose the colour since she was possibly the only one who would be using it.

All the old furniture was piled up in the hallway, most of it although old, circ 1950s was still of very good quality. 'Oh My,' said Julie Clutterbuck,' seeing all her furniture stacked up on the first floor bedroom hallway, when she went up to see how the girls were getting on. 'You have had a clearout haven't you.' Dorothy saw at once that Julie was a little put out, clearly having offered Rosemary accommodation, Julie was not expecting her old furniture to be discarded.

Dorothy ever the diplomat said, 'Sorry Julie, we thought you wouldn't mind, since Rosemary might be staying with you for some time it seemed sensible that we should furnish it in a way that suited her character, and you know as I do she's a bit dippy, I thought your old furniture grand as it is, was, well a bit dark, and if anything we all need to brighten up Rosemary's life in one way or the other.' Dorothy's tactics worked, Julie saw at once that a woman in her thirties would hardly want to live in a room that echoed of the past, and as she recollected, the furnishings were those of the late Rev Sudbury not hers or Nigel's. Rosemary came into the hall just as Dorothy and Julie had finished discussing the old Vicars furniture. 'Hello Julie, glad you've come up we were wondering what to do with all this stuff?' exclaimed Rosemary tactless as ever. Julie said, 'If you can you get someone to move it down to the cellar, I'll see if Nigel can make a bit of room for it, I don't think we should chuck it out since it seems to be in pretty good condition to me, even if it is old.'

A couple of days later, Nigel Clutterbuck was down in the cellar, it was the first time since they moved in a few years ago that Nigel had even been down there. Being not so agile these days, he had left any forage's into the cellar to Julie, and she herself felt uneasy down there, possibly due to its former priory associations. Where on earth could he find room down here for an old double bed, and all the other furnishings that Rosemary had basically chucked out as rubbish, he wanted to send them to a charity shop, but Julie argued that in due course surely Rosemary would move on, and take her new furniture with her, and then this furniture could be moved back and the room could serve as an extra guest bedroom as it had in the past.

The cellar was full to the brim, Nigel started as best he could to push the larger items against the walls. A lot of the stuff was really old junk, with boxes and stacks of old church files etc, he glanced at some of the aged church paperwork circ 1940s and thought he might get someone to go through it some day, it might disclose a bit about the more recent history of the church. As he cleared things away he found some shelves, and on one was a stone effigy of a religious person.

Nigel called Julie down to see his find; there were other stone relics on the shelf alongside it. 'It looks as if it belongs to the Norman Priory,' said Julie. I'll call Rosemary and Dorothy down they might know what it means.

Dorothy and Rosemary stood gazing at the effigy, 'It's a Norman Bishop by the look of it,' exclaimed an excited Dorothy. 'Look,' said Rosemary, 'Theres some mosaic floor tiles on the shelf as well.' They found several other artefacts of an ecclesiastical nature on another shelf. 'These must be all from the Norman Fitzroy Priory.

The Effigy of a Norman Bishop

I bet the Rev Sudbury found them scattered around the church when he was the churches incumbent,' suggested Dr Clutterbuck. 'But why didn't he take them to the museum in Reedsthorpe,' asked Rosemary. 'Probably because the museum did not get really known until Jack Wilkinson took it on, we had lived in Reedsthorpe most of our lives and never knew it existed till he started promoting it, and setting up a Trust at the bequest of the leader of the Lincolnshire County Council,' Julie said, 'Tell you what Nigel, if you can put them in some boxes I'll drop them off at the museum this afternoon, I bet you've forgotten its my Drama Club meeting in Reedsthorpe at five.'

Nigel sighed, wondering what to do with himself, tonight, as Dorothy helped him pack the artefacts. Rosemary and Dorothy took the artefacts and put them in the boot of Julie's car. Then Rosemary headed down to the Crows Roost Inn to find Len the church sexton and general handyman, hoping to get him to help get all that old furniture down to the cellar, for the price of a couple of pints, while Dorothy went back upstairs to fetch some of the smaller items down.

Chapter 11

The Angry Tall Thin Man

One evening, Geoffrey and Sophie were walking along the Promenade towards the Eden Cinema in Reedsthorpe, to see the final Harry Potter film. When Sophie suddenly grabbed Geoffrey's arm and said, 'Isn't that Tony, that Nurse Martha's son?' Just a few yards in front of them, a teenage boy was walking along with a tall thin man who was wearing a combat jacket, the man was carrying a large battered old leather bag 'Do you know your right, it is Tony,' said Geoffrey. 'Who's that he's with? I'm sure he's a bit familiar, I'm sure I've seen him before,' said Sophie.

'Look we'd better hurry along the film starts in fifteen minutes, don't want to miss the start,' said Geoffrey as he took her arm and speeded up their walking pace. As they began to catch up with Tony and the man, Geoffrey slowed down and pulled Sophie back, 'It's him, the man in the Hide, remember the angry man.' 'How could I forget, it was very frightening I thought he was going to hit you,' said Sophie. 'So did I actually,' replied Geoffrey. 'But you didn't seem to be frightened,' said Sophie. 'Well perhaps I was trying to impress you a bit, we weren't going out then were we,' he admitted.

'Look, Sophie I've just thought, do you remember that every one thought that Tony told some one about the Gyrfalcon, and that was why we were invaded by the twitchers.' 'Of course no one will forget that in a hurry,' she exclaimed. 'I think we should follow them, they haven't noticed us yet,' suggested Geoffrey. 'But what about Harry Potter,' protested Sophie, knowing that Geoffrey would be impossible until he found out what the tall thin man was up to and that the film would have to wait. They followed the two now at some distance, so far they had not been noticed. Along the promenade there were several two sided shelters, with seating, one side overlooking the beach the other the road and terraces of guesthouses. The tall thin man and Tony went and sat on the beach side of the first one they came to, they were in deep conversation, when Geoffrey and Sophie un-noticed caught up with them and quietly sat on the seats directly behind them. There was a graffiti covered perspex partition separating them. 'Right,' said Geoffrey, 'We have to be careful, if Tony sees us, he might tell the man who we are; if that happens get ready to run.' Sophie put her arm round Geoffrey's shoulder and cuddled up, whispering, ' If we do this they won't bother us, we look just like any other couple.' 'Good idea,' whispered Geoffrey. They tried to listen to what the man and Tony were talking about, but their voices were hushed. Sophie glanced round carefully and saw through the Perspex partition that the man was showing something to Tony.

The man raised his voice as he excitedly said to Tony, 'That's what we need lots of them next year, I can pay you well.' His voice then lowered back to a whisper. Sophie was searching in her bag. 'What are you doing?' asked Geoffrey. 'Shush, you'll see,' she said, as she took out her make up mirror and carefully pretended to do up her make up. She was sitting too low down to adjust the mirror so she could see what the thin man and Tony were looking at. She promptly stood up, saying loudly in a dialect that Geoffrey had never heard before, 'You have mucked up my make up, I will have to fix it up again you moron.' As she did so she set the mirror at an angle and clearly saw the man putting something back in his bag, it looked like an egg. She grabbed Geoffrey and ushered him out of the shelter and back along the promenade the way they had come, 'Quick, don't look back, I think they have seen us, we need to get out of sight in case Geoffrey recognises us.' They ducked into the amusement arcade, and pretended to play the machines. When no one had come after them, Geoffrey crept to the arcades doorway and looked back down towards the shelter they had been sitting in. The tall thin man was still there standing next to Tony talking, but looking directly down towards the arcade, he couldn't see Geoffrey, because he was only just peeking out, and there was a flurry of youngsters coming into the arcade at the same time, as others were leaving it. He saw the tall thin man shake his head and then cross the road heading the other way. Tony started walking down towards the arcade, then suddenly crossed the road and headed into a side street, and up the hill to his mothers Martha's new flat.

They were too late by far to see Harry Potter now, but the excitement of seeing the angry tall thin man again and his knowing Tony was quite unexpected if not a little scary. 'We need to get back and tell

Mr Taylor, he was talking to me about egg collecting and the law, earlier this year.' They caught the next bus home and went straight round to Mr Taylor's bungalow.

Shelia Taylor opened the door, as Geoffrey uttered the words, 'Egg Collectors got to see Mr Taylor urgently.' Shelia invited them both in, and sat them in the lounge overlooking the back garden and their new pond, that they had put in after reading Charlie Dimmock's book, ***Every Garden Needs a Water Feature*** that Shelia had bought a signed copy of, from Charlie herself at last years Church Spring Fete. While they sat admiring the pond, Shelia telephoned the Clutterbuck's house. 'Sorry Bill but Geoffrey and Sophie are here something about egg collectors.' Shelia went back into the lounge, 'Bill won't be long he's coming home now he was at the Rectory. Can I get any of you anything, drink perhaps?' 'No thanks anyway, just want to tell Mr Taylor what we have just found out, and I must get home,' said a smiling Sophie. 'I wouldn't mind a coffee butted in Geoffrey I'm not in a hurry.' Geoffrey's coffee arrived just as Bill Taylor came through the front door.

After they were all settled, Geoffrey told about how they had met this tall thin angry man down at the Hide at Sprig Point Nature Reserve earlier in the year, photographing the Bitterns. Sophie then related to Bill and Shelia how they saw the same man with Tony earlier this evening in Reedsthorpe and how they had followed them, and overheard the man telling Tony he wanted a lot of these next year, and that Sophie's using her make up mirror thought she saw them looking at a birds egg, and how she thought the man had seen her and they got away and hid in the arcade. 'Well that's quite a story, and it fits in with something I was told about earlier this year.' Bill then told them how a clutch of Bitterns eggs had been stolen down at Sprig Point in the spring, and suspicions had fallen on a tall thin man wearing combat trousers and jacket that had been seen hanging about the reserve at the time. He had to be warned off the reserve several times, and then seemed to have vanished all together; the warden's thought he had moved away.

'So could it be that if this man was now known to the Wardens at Sprig Point, they will have notified all the other reserves along the coast to look out for him?' Shelia suggested. Sophie quick as a flash cottoned on, 'So he needs some one else to do his dirty work collecting eggs, that must be where Tony comes in, and they are planning their egg collecting missions for next year.' 'Bravo,' shouted out Bill and Shelia in unison. 'That's some bright girl friend you have there, young Geoffrey, hope some of it rubs off on you,' said Bill laughingly. They all rolled about laughing, even Geoffrey didn't take offence, he was proud that Mr and Mrs Taylor now saw him as Sophie's proper boyfriend.

The next day Bill rang the regional headquarters of the RSPB at Boston. 'We'll get our Investigations Officer onto it, but its unlikely that much can be done until the breeding season begins next year, if we raid his home now he's likely to have sold off most of the eggs he may have stolen this year, and he will have been warned off too soon. We need to catch him in the act of taking, or receiving and passing on the eggs. A few eggs in his house won't get much of a fine or conviction.'

The RSPB put out a description of the man, and sent it to all the reserves in Lincolnshire and Norfolk all the wardens and reserve managers were instructed to just record every where he was seen over the winter months, it would allow them to work out which birds he intended to target next season. Bill said he would find out where the boy Tony was living providing he was not to be targeted, and that his name would be protected for his mother's sake.

Bill hoped to meet the Investigations Officer to see how Tony could be safe guarded; he knew Tony was an innocent pawn in a very dangerous game. He wanted to tell Martha, but decided after Shelia talked to him to leave it to the professionals, other wise he could jeopardise any proposed RSPB operation. All they could do was to keep quiet till next year, but keep their ears to the ground. Bill made it clear to Sophie and Geoffrey that they must not make any attempt to find the man again, or follow Tony it could be actually life threatening, the money that could change hands in egg collecting deals was enormous, and some people would not hesitate to kill to protect their interests.

A subdued Geoffrey and Sophie went home, Sophie to the shop and Geoffrey to his parents house on the green just a few hundred yards away both wondering exactly what had they walked into.

The Reedsthorpe Museum Robbery

Two weeks later Jack Wilkinson was in bed, when his phone rang, he glanced at his side table clock and registered the time as 2.15 am. 'Hello is that Mr Wilkinson.' 'Yes this is Jack who's that?' 'Sorry to disturb you this early, but this is Dennis of Security Systems Reedsthorpe; I'm afraid your Museum alarm is going off, we have a man heading down there now, could you get down to meet him with the keys?' 'Yes of course I'll be ten minutes'. Jack arrived at the Museum, which was just off the main street in Reedsthorpe near the Promenade. It was two terraced houses joined as one to house mainly, local history memorabilia, some archaeology, and Alf Pritchard's recently donated war artefacts and documentation. Other than this on the top floor was a very small Natural History Collection donated many years ago by the late Edward Biggles, a butcher by trade, but a well known local naturalist and in his younger days long before birds eggs were protected, an avid egg collector.

The security man was there before Jack had arrived, and had carried out an external check of the premises, he reported to Jack that he could find no evidence of a break in, or forced entry. Jack followed the Security man, as they did another quick check round. 'Well must be a false alarm, but its never happened before,' Jack told the man. 'I think we had better check inside just in case,' advised the security man. They both inspected each room in turn, but nothing appeared to be amiss. 'Is your security up to date Mr Wilkinson, your alarm may be ready for updating,' asked the security man. 'To be honest we don't actually have much of great value here, there's no art or anything like that,' he replied. 'Could any one else have been in here working late?' asked the man. 'No, and only one of my volunteers has the other key, and she's a nurse usually working night shifts at Reesdsthorpe Infirmary. The security officer went back to his depot, and Jack back to bed putting all thoughts of the matter out of his head.

The next morning Jack opened up the museum as usual, soon after one of his volunteers arrived, Cedric a retired naval officer who had taken on the responsibility for looking after the war collection. 'Morning Cedric, would you do me a favour while I sort out the post, the alarm went off last night, I got called out but we checked round and everything seemed okay, but I think we need to check round again, can you start on the top floor, and I'll start down here when I've finished this.' Cedric happily headed up the narrow stairs to get started. It wasn't long before Cedric came back down, 'Jack you'd better come and see this.' Cedric led Jack up to the small Natural History Room; they went over to the glass cabinets containing Edward Biggles 1950s egg collection. All the cabinets were empty, and unlocked. 'But why, who could have taken them, I came in here early this morning with the security man, but I didn't actually look in the cabinets.' 'Well some ones been in here, and furthermore they had a cabinet key to get in,' said Cedric. 'Quick lets check the key box at reception,' cried out Jack. Down at the reception desk Jack took out the key box from the desk drawer, and counted out the keys, they were all, there including the egg cabinet key. 'Must be an inside job,' suggested Cedric. Jack sat down at his desk and tried to work things out. 'But the alarm went off at about 2.10 am, so that must be when the eggs were taken, and only one person has another key to get in the museum, and that's nurse Martha. But Martha works night shift so it couldn't have been her. All day long Jack and Cedric tried to work out the various scenarios that might have been played out to affect such a robbery. 'Should we call the police,' asked Cedric when they had failed to solve the riddle. 'No I don't want our volunteers to think any of them could be involved or suspected, there has to be a logical solution, lets keep it quiet for now, and listen out for anyone selling eggs in the vicinity,' said Jack.

A few days later Jack had met up with Dr Clutterbuck in the Crows Roost Inn at Melton-Uppbury to discuss a future topic for a meeting of the Melton-Uppbury Historical Group. He was telling Nigel about the museum break in, and about the missing eggs, when Bill Taylor and his wife Shelia who were sitting at the next table having dinner, leaned over, 'Sorry, couldn't help over hearing you mention missing birds eggs,' Bill said. 'Yes, actually you might be able to help, who would want to take a collection of motley old birds eggs?' asked Jack in a whispered tone. 'Egg collectors, of course there's always a market for rare birds eggs, in fact since its been illegal to collect them since the late fifties, any birds egg rare or not will fetch a good price these days,' replied

Bill. Shelia piped in, 'And we know there's one egg collector knocking about in Reedsthorpe or at least there was up to a few weeks ago.' 'Yes the RSPB are looking into it, but since the nesting seasons not till next spring, there's not much they can do at the moment,' added Bill. 'Haven't you noticed anyone taking a special interest in the eggs of late,' asked Nigel. 'Well to be honest no one much seems to go up to the Natural History Room these days, only young Tony sometimes, in fact he came in with a friend last week,' said Jack. 'You mean Martha the Nurses son Tony,' blurted out Bill. 'Yes, but he's just a kid, and his mother helps us out a lot especially with the paper work,' replied Jack. 'Look there's too many ears listening in here, so we have just about finished our dinner, so why don't you both come up to our bungalow and I think we can solve this puzzle quite easily.'

Back at Bill and Shelia's home the whole story came out. The angry tall thin man, fitted the description Jack gave of Tony's friend who he took to see the museums Natural History Collection. Geoffrey and Sophie's encounter with the angry tall thin man, and their chanced seeing him again in the company of Tony in Reedsthorpe, apparently planning an egg stealing expedition for next spring. It was clear that young Tony had got hold of his mother's museum key, while she was at work and on his own or with the tall thin man entered the museum in the early hours and located the egg cabinet key and removed all the eggs. Clearly the matter had to be referred to the Police and the

RSPB, after all it was a robbery, and using keys or not it was an illegal entry.

Jack and Bill decided to speak to Tony's mother Martha before they reported the matter to the authorities. They met at the museum on the Saturday morning, and explained what had happened and how it appeared that her son Tony had got involved with this very dangerous man. Martha admitted she had been worried for some time about Tony, that was why she got him to come with her on that gyrfalcon bird watch earlier in the year, and she had actually encouraged him to take a bit of an interest in birds, and even got him to come and see the museums Natural History Room. 'And the other week when I was looking after the museum myself, Tony asked if he could hold one of the eggs, he had never touched one before, and certainly hadn't seen one in the wild, so I found the cabinet key, and allowed him to hold some of them, he got quite excited about it, so I thought it was a good thing,' admitted a distraught Martha, 'Its all my fault, I have to work night shift and Tony's left on his own, and in the day I have to try and get some sleep, that bloody x husband of mine never shows his bloody face.'

Jack and Bill didn't know where to put themselves, but it was clear that the tall thin man had manipulated Tony to do his bidding. Jack asked Martha, 'How do you think Tony got to know this man.' 'Oh, he told me a good few weeks ago that he'd met this really nice bird watcher, who was an expert on rare birds, he told Tony he could teach him a lot, and he might even make some money out of the hobby when he got better at it,' Martha explained. They were now faced with a very difficult situation, if they told the police, or the RSPB everything, Tony might get arrested and taken to court for breaking and entering. No there had to be another way, they needed to talk to Tony, as did his mother of course. Martha rang Tony on his mobile. 'Hi mum what's up, you don't often bother to ring me?' 'Look Tony I'm at the museum we need a bit of help and you're the only one who can do it.' Tony gasped, what was going on, it was at least a week since he had taken his friend to the museum to get those old eggs, he wondered if he had been rumbled, he tried to get out of going, 'Can't someone else help mum I'm busy?' She said, 'No Tony you must come now, if you don't it will make my life even more difficult than it is already.' 'Okay mum.'

Ten minutes later a very subdued Tony tried to act is if nothing was amiss as he walked up to the reception desk where Martha was waiting. 'Wait a minute she said as she closed the front door and put the closed sign up. 'Look we know what you have done, and you have to tell us honestly what you and your so called friend have been up to.' She then took Tony to see Jack and Bill in the Natural History Room. After a lot of excuses and blustering from Tony, Martha shouted, 'Tony I know when your covering things up, your bloody dad was just the same tell us everything you know.' Jack said kindly, 'Look Tony we already have a good idea about what's been going on, we know you must have used your mothers key, so unless you intend to tell us your own mothers an egg stealer and we have to call the police in you'd better tell the truth.'

The possibility that his mum might get dragged into his robbery was too much, and he broke down and confessed to everything, starting with the twitchers invasion, it turns out that after Tony had told his so called friend, the tall thin man had told some of his contacts, one of whom must have known Sinclair, and told him about the gyrfalcon sighting. The tall thin man had hoped to attract them to the village, and distract the Priory Birders from their watch stations whilst he crept up to the mound where Geoffrey and Margaret had seen the bird on the fens, to see if there were any eggs, he had anticipated that with the twitchers all over the village, he could get away with it without being seen, that the watchers at station 2 would have been called back, to avoid the invasion, but he was wrong because a young lady saw him creeping up to the mound, and she shouted out and he had to escape down by the river near the pub. His plan had gone completely wrong, and he cursed that young woman who was Tony's mums nurse friend Margaret. Tony had been telling him where everyone was on his mobile from the café where he and his mother had been watching out for the bird.

There guess as to what the man intended Tony to do next year was correct, Tony told them the plan was for him to steal avocet eggs next year from the reserves down the coast, because his friend would be recognised, whereas a teenage boy was a much less suspect. The break in to steal all the museum eggs was so the man could sell them to egg collectors in the Midlands, and Tony told them that the man who Tony knew as Michael still had trays of eggs, that he had collected last season where he lived, which he was negotiating the sale of. 'So where does this Michael live?' asked Bill. 'He's got a rented caravan on the Sunnyside Site; the one just passed the Sprig Point Reserve. 'Very convenient,' said Bill. Jack said, 'Well what do we do now?' Martha pleaded, 'Please don't report Tony to the police, he'll end up like his dad, Tony is a good kid really, and its that mans fault, putting all these stupid ideas in his head.' Bill said, 'I'll tell you what we have to do, first I must get the RSPB Investigations Officer up here, then we can talk through the options, if we play things carefully Tony could be the hero of the hour, and that man Michael put out of action for a bit.' Jack said, 'I'll go along with that, I don't want Tony getting a record at his age, it'll ruin his young life, we have all done some stupid things in our time I'm sure.'

A couple of days later, the RSPB Officer met Jack, Bill, Tony, and Martha at the museum. He was very understanding, and suggested that if Tony could perhaps on the off chance, call in to see this Michael and get him to show him those drawers of eggs again, just to be sure they were still there, they could do a raid on the caravan as a joint RSPB/Police operation. Martha protested that Tony might be in danger, and she did not intend that he was to get hurt just for the sake of a few birds eggs. Tony had no such reservations, if he could make amends for his wrongdoing, and not get arrested for the break in, he would do it. Two weeks later Tony knocked on the caravan door, having phoned the mobile number the man had given him. As he opened the door he said, 'Right Tony what have you got for me?' As the door was closed from prying eyes Tony handed Michael an egg that Jack had found in a drawer that had not been taken, it was the egg of the Great Northern Diver. Michael took it greedily, he knew someone who was looking for just such an egg, to complete his Diver egg collection. He pulled open one of the concealed drawers from under a bed and placed it gently between the eggs of a Black Throated Diver and a Red Throated Diver. Tony said, 'Can I see the others, I'd love my own collection eventually?' 'The tall thin man said, 'If you keep helping me I'll make sure you get one, but it takes time.' As Tony stepped down from the caravan steps he glimpsed the shadow of the RSPB man, watching from behind a tree. Tony pretended not to see him, as he knew Michael was watching him, he got on his bike and rode off the site.

He met up with Bill in the lay by of the Sprig Point Nature reserve, and informed him that the tall thin man still had most of the eggs under his caravan bed. Bill phoned the RSPB man who was watching the caravan. His phone vibrated in his pocket, since he had put his phone on silent mode, 'He's still got them all under the beds in drawers.' 'Right can you send my assistant John down here we need to stake the place out for a couple of days, don't want that Michael bloke to associate Tony's visit with our raid, but we have to be sure he doesn't move the eggs before we go in.' 'Okay John's on his way, but he's coming down through the fields so it'll be about twenty minutes or so before he reaches you.' I've sent Tony home, and I'm off myself keep me up to date won't you, goodnight.'

Bill drove through Reedstorpe just in time to see the rear light of Tony's bike disappear up a side street. He thought to himself, I wonder if we might steer that young man in the direction of a career in conservation instead of crime. Before he left Reedsthorpe, he stopped off at the hospital to let Martha know that her son Tony had done a good job, and impressed the RSPB men, and that he had just passed him on his bike going up the lane to her flat. A much-relieved nurse went back to her ward that evening, whistling a merry tune to herself.

Two weeks later the police assisted the RSPB officers to raid the caravan site, they searched several other caravans, before actually getting to the tall thin mans van, a ploy to let him know that no one had actually led them directly to his caravan, an extra protective measure for Tony's sake.

In due course the angry tall thin man known as Michael appeared in court and was given three years, since it was his fifth egg stealing offence, no charges were laid in respect of the theft from the museum, those eggs were quietly returned to Jack by the RSPB.

Chapter 12

The Monks get a Christian Burial

Zoe as promised had all the monks and their family bones returned to the village. In all ten male adults, four adult females, eight children between the ages of three and fifteen and two babies had been recovered from the Clutterbucks garden. Every one had been murdered and their bodies mutilated. It had taken the Cambridge Laboratory forensic team three months to finally work out how many bodies there were and what pieces fitted where. A report was prepared which gave cause of death, illnesses each person had suffered in life and evidence of any deformity recorded.

The knowledge gained from the investigation proved to be very important, it was the first real evidence that could be physically seen, of the butchery of the Vikings on early English Christians. The Museum and University authorities desperately wanted to hang on to the bones for future research, but the formidable might of the Rev Rosemary Fitter, Archaeologist Zoe Hartington, Mike Hartington, Dr Nigel Clutterbuck, Jack Wilkinson of the Reedsthorpe Museum, Gerald Parker, and many others along with several petitions pressured the authorities to eventually relinquish the bones. The locals of Melton-Uppbury were convinced that unless the bones of the monks and their families were laid to rest, and received a Christian burial they would continue to haunt the village, a prospect no one wanted.

The Monks deaths Explained

The findings of the museum specialists had added to Nigel's grief about the decapitation of the five year old child. The Melton-Uppbury Historical Group held a meeting to which Zoe Hartington and Jack Wilkinson were invited in the Village Hall. The full horror of the Viking Massacre of the monks and their defenceless families back in the 800s was graphically described and dramatically shown on a computer reconstruction of the events that led up to their deaths, set up by some of Zoe's colleagues. Nigel left the meeting early not being able to face up to what had in part taken place in his garden about 1200 years ago. Julie stuck it out and stayed on at the meeting but would not handle the bones showing clear evidence of the actions of the Vikings double edged swords and axes.

The experts having reviewed the evidence, including a site visit to the Rectory and beach, and having seen all the places where people had seen the ghostly forms of long dead monks concluded that the Viking attack happened circ 810. The wooden Saxon Priory was burnt down about the same time. The monks had raised the alarm when they saw a long ship sailing down the coast from the River Humber, when some of them were quietly walking northwards along the beach towards the river outlet where Fred Allsops Boatyard now stands, in prayerful contemplation. They turned and ran as seen in a ghostly re-enactment witnessed by Silas Pestell, down the beach to the cut by the lay by, onto the main road and down to Church lane as witnessed by Harry Weatherspoon, both sightings that took place last year. Clearly the ghostly apparitions were shouting out warnings to everyone who lived in the priory or around it, and gathering women and children with them on the way. The Prior must had some warnings of the possibility of attack, some time before allowing them time to bury the priory treasures in the Dunes. But when the attack actually took place it took them completely by surprise. Another longboat must have come up from the south, because the Vikings must have got hold of some of the community on the beach and on the dunes, before they could get to the relative safety of the church, which explains the screams and cries of men women and children heard by Mrs Barrhead some two years ago. The rest of the, would be escapees only got as far as the present Rectory garden, when they were caught. They must have all been trying to reach the old Anglo Saxon Church. Some time later a few members of the community who might have got away or peoples from some of the small hamlets in land, on the fens; must have found the mutilated bodies and buried them close to where they fell.

St Guthlac's Church Funeral Preparations

The Rev Rosemary Fitter arrived at an autumn evening Special Meeting of the Parochial Church Council at St Guthlac's church. Also in attendance was Mrs Bottomly in the Chair, Gerald Parker, Col Smith-Fitzroy, Mrs Alderton, and invited guests Archaeologist Zoe Hartington nee Lake and Dr and Mrs Clutterbuck. Apologies were duly noted of committee members unable to attend. Tonight's meeting was convened to discuss and work out the best plan for conducting a funeral for the remains of the dead monks, women, and children that had been recovered from the Rectory garden a few months ago. Mr Parker stood up and addressed the meeting:

'Well ladies and gentlemen this is rather a sad occasion, but also exciting we are here to discuss the disposal or rather internment of all the bones that have been dug up from Nigel and Julies garden.'

The Rectory Garden

Mrs Bottomly immediately stood up and shouted at Mr Parker,

'Excuse me! Mr Parker this is not a Parish Council Meeting, and I am the Chair of this committee if you don't mind.'

An embarrassed Gerald Parker turned red in the face, realising what he had just done. It had always been in Gerald's nature to take charge of things, he was indeed a natural born community leader, but this was a church committee and Mrs Bottomly was is chairperson, and in reality for a number of years she had been the churches mainstay. Since the recent appointment of Rosemary Fitter to that of full time Rector to St Guthlac's, Mrs Bottomly had felt a little bit put out, because Rosemary was now doing many of the tasks, that had previously been done by herself. But to have Gerald Parker take over her role as chairperson was more than a soul could bear.

'Oh I do most sincerely apologise Mrs Bottomly, I'm sorry, I'm afraid I got a little bit mixed up being chair of so many other committees, I simply was not thinking, Sorry.'

The other committee members and invited guests wriggled uncomfortably in their chairs, when old Mrs Alderton stood up and said,

'Look here I'm sure Mr Parker was not trying to take over your job, Mrs Bottomly we all know how well you have kept this church going through the bad times. Mr Parker has apologised, so its up to you to see how we all feel about this important and difficult and indeed sensitive matter, so what do you want us to do.'

Peace prevailed and a course of action was planned, incorporating the wishes of the committee and the invited guests. It was clear that the Finds had been a major local news item, and that although the remains were to be reburied in accordance with Christian Tradition; they had provided the scientists, archaeologists and historians with a lot of data, and casts of the bones had been made for further studies. However as Col Smith-Fitzroy had pointed out members of the public had not been able to see them, which seemed a bit unfair, especially to the locals, who had not attended the recent meeting of the Historical Group.

So it was decided that since each of the sets of bones had been sorted and classified according to sex, and age, and DNA tests had enabled the scientists to ensure that each bone was put with bones that matched the profile of that individual, and boxed accordingly, that the public should have the opportunity to view them prior to burial.

The church committee agreed that the boxed remains should be laid out on trestle tables at the back of the church for a period of four weeks and that the church should be open between 10 am to 4 pm for visitors. Zoe Hartington agreed to write out a short profile for each of the individuals in the boxes, so that visitors could understand and see whom these people might have been and how they had each been slaughtered. As Rosemary pointed out Christians had always been persecuted; from the very origins of the church there were those opposed to it and wanted it destroyed and replaced to suit the needs of its destroyers. Col Smith-Fitzroy was quick to point out how small communities of Christians were being slaughtered and even crucified today in various parts of the world.

October was selected as the month that the remains should be on show in the church. Rosemary made it clear that visitors should see their opportunity to view the remains not so much as a curiosity, or morbid exhibition, but it should be viewed as an opportunity for people to pay homage to a few early Christians who gave their lives for their Faith.

They jointly agreed that a memorial should be erected to these Martyrs on the roadside outside the Rectory, for Martyrs they indeed were. There could be little doubt that the events of this year would put St Guthlac's Church on the map, and bring a new kind of tourism to the village of Melton-Uppbury. Dr Clutterbuck and his wife clearly were worried about what might happen, would they find people climbing over their garden walls with metal detectors looking for more monastic treasure, would they have to sell up they wondered. Mrs Bottomly as she was closing the meeting said, 'We have to respect Dr Clutterbuck and Mrs Clutterbucks concerns and future privacy, so I would like to suggest that we distort the truth a little.' Zoe said, 'I very much agree with Mrs Bottomly, but how can we possibly do it?' 'I know,' piped in, 'James Smith-Fitzroy, how many people actually know the bones were found in the Rectory Garden?' 'Well actually only those involved in the actual dig, and us here round this table I think,' suggested Julie Clutterbuck. Nigel then came up with a brain wave. 'I've got it, think about it where have most people seen the monks ghosts?' 'On the beach and in and near the dunes of course,' said Edith Barrhead as she came belatedly into the church meeting, catching the last question. 'That's it then, said Gerald, 'let's sort of hint that at least some of the bones were found near where most people saw the apparitions, that's not really untrue since the Rectory is not too far away only in fact a few minutes walk.'

Rosemary asked to have a quiet word with Zoe outside and asked every one if they would mind waiting for a few minutes. On their return Zoe addressed the meeting, 'I think Rosemary has come up with a great idea, which will enable us to give people the impression that the beach and the dunes was where most if not all the bones were found.'

The plan was simple, the actual Funeral Service could begin on the beach, or actually exactly where the sightings in the main took place in the dunes. The Boxed remains would be carried there from the church by the locals; there was little weight or bulk to the remains so that would not present them with any problems. The boxes would be laid side by side on the ground as Rosemary read out the beginning of the office for the dead. Then the boxed remains would be conveyed again by the locals from the beach, down the main road and onto church lane, accompanied by the ritual singing of Psalms 39 and 90, and in fact following the same route that Silas and Harry had seen the ghostly monks take a few months previously. Up at the church the boxed remains would be lined before the Altar, Mrs Bottomly could do the Reading, the lesson taken from the 15th chapter of St Pauls letter to the Corinthians.

The final act would be the burial in the church graveyard. They would have to work out exactly where they were to be buried since space was at a premium, but Rosemary wanted it to be as near to the church as possible, preferably on the south side.

A few weeks later the day of the funeral came around. A burial plot had been found close to the south side of the church very close to the door archway. Len the sexton had dug side by side, fourteen plots each three by two feet, to accommodate the bones of the fourteen adults, these were just big enough to do the job. Then he dug eight plots of slightly varying sizes for the children's remains, and one small plot in which it had been agreed that the two babies should be placed.

The showing of the remains of these martyrs in the church prior to the funeral; had brought hundreds of visitors. It was in fact the only fully proven Viking massacre of innocent Christians ever found in the British Isles. Television News crews had camped along Church Lane, filming the visitors, including some famous names. Some visitors went away claiming they had miraculous cures as a result of just touching the bones; a practice that a number of volunteers including Sophie Weatherspoon and Geoffrey Thompson, Mrs

Bottomly and Mrs Alderton, directed by The Rev Fitter had tried to prevent.

The beach was crowded on the cold and windy day in October when the funeral took place. Nigel and Julie thwarted an attempt made to steal one of the boxes of bones. A group of selected locals twenty-four in all, were to each collect a box from the church and in procession led by Rosemary take them down Church Lane past the Rectory down to the beach. Nigel and Julie stood at their gate and looked on solemnly as the procession passed, the last box was being carried by and Julie whispered to Nigel, 'Who's that Nigel? 'Who's in the box?' he replied. 'Don't be stupid Nigel, who is it carrying the box.

They slowly followed the procession as it turned north towards the beach cut and lay by. As they did so the man Julie asked Nigel about, did an about turn and started running back down the main road towards the Crows Roost Inn Car Park. Nigel and Julie gave chase, just in time to see James Smith-Fitzroy and his barmaid Helen walking out of the car park to catch up with the procession. They faced an anguished middle-aged overweight little man racing towards them carrying a cardboard box. 'Stop him, James he's stealing a box of bones!' shouted Julie. Nigel had slowed down he couldn't keep up. The man swept by James ducking a blow from Helen as he did so. He ran into the car park and was desperately trying to open the door to an old ford car, but with trying to balance the box he dropped his keys, which were quickly seized by James. James took the box and gave it to Helen and said, 'Take this as quick as you can and join up with the procession, I'll deal with this guy, turning round he was just in time to see the little man running down the track towards the river. James didn't see any point in exerting himself, and he did not want to miss the funeral, so he let all the cars tyres down, and took a quick note of the registration number entering it onto his mobile phone as he walked up to join the others he gave the police a quick call.

As Helen carried the box back up the main road, she met up with an anxious puffing and panting Alf Pritchard, who had just been up to the church. He cried out, 'I've just been to collect that box, I overslept, but everyone had already left the church when I got there, and there were no boxes left.' Helen quickly told Alf what had happened, as she handed the box to him. He was just in time to place the box with the others in the dunes as Rosemary began the service:

I am the resurrection and the life, saith the Lord: he that believeth in me, though he were dead, yet shall he live: and whosoever liveth and believeth in me shall never die.

Read out Rosemary from the Book of Common Prayer, as she looked over the boxes of the Martyrs bones, lying side by side in the middle of the sand dunes. She then gave the sign of the cross over them and sprinkled a little Holy Water. The whole area was crowded with spectators; many people had tears in their eyes when they saw the two smallest boxes containing the remains of the babies. At the back of the crowd Nigel wept uncontrollably comforted by Julie.

The funeral procession went up to the church, as it passed the Rectory, Julie and Nigel slipped quietly into their garden. By the time the procession got to the church many of the outsider non-locals had wandered off, some heading to the Crows Roost Inn, not knowing that James had shut up shop until after the funeral as a mark of respect to the dead.

Man that was born of a woman hath but a short time to live, and is full of misery. He cometh up, and is cut down, like a flower; he fleet hast it were a shadow, and never continueth in one stay.

Rosemary's voice echoed around the quiet churchyard, as the boxes of bones were carefully lowered into their respective plots. At the end of the service, several including Mrs Alderton and Mrs Clutterbuck who had a short time ago settled Nigel in his conservatory chair with a stiff whisky and returned in time to see the small box of babies bones being covered with soil, stood in silent prayer with tears rolling down their faces.

This small group of sombre mourners led by the Rev Rosemary Fitter arm in arm with Col James Smith-Fitzroy slowly walked through the churchyard gateway onto Church Lane, heading to the Crows Roost Inn for a Wake that James had left his barmaid Helen to set up. As they came down the lane, they encountered a thick mist that had been blown over from the dunes, for a moment it engulfed them all, but no one was perturbed, in fact they all felt a strange but wonderful calm come upon them. Rosemary spoke out, 'Jesus is with us.' They all stopped walking and felt the Spirit around them.

Then the mist slowly blew over to the church and settled over the graves of the monks, women, and children they had just buried. As they looked back towards the church they watched the mist disperse, and they all saw a group of cowled figures, with their arms protectively wrapped around four women, holding babies, and children, all within a circle which seemed to be now lit up by a powerful beam of sunlight that had broken through the clouded sky. The faces on the figures were obscure but seemingly smiling, a little boy of about five years old held up his hand waving to them, as all the apparitions, and the mist slowly dispersed.

The small group of mourners stood mesmerised in the lane in wonderment and awe: they all quietly encircled each other as Rosemary led them in reciting the Lords Prayer. 'Its over,' said Edith. Even James, with a lifetime of scepticism about God, and the church generally, felt emotionally and spiritually moved.

A few days later a police officer called on James at the pub. The man who had tried to steal the box of bones still had not returned for his car. 'Well Col Smith we have traced the owner of the car, it turns out that he had heard about some of the alleged miraculous cures that some people had claimed occurred after touching the bones when they were on show in your church.' James said, 'Well what did he intend to do with them?'

'That's the sad thing, it turns out the mans wife has an incurable form of cancer, and only has a few months left to live.' James read the constables next words for him, 'So he thought this was his only chance of saving her.' 'Yes sadly that's the case,' said the constable. James said, 'If you can give me the mans address I'll, get his car back to him, in fact I'll take the Rev Fitter with me, she might just be able to give the couple a bit of assurance and support, if they aren't getting any from any one else.' 'I'm sure that would be the right thing to do, but I'll have to check it out first if you don't mind,' the constable replied.

The Onset of Winter

As autumn turns to winter the residents of the village of Melton-Uppbury have once again settled down to the quiet life, the exciting events of spring and summer are fading into distant memories. There are no more ghostly apparitions of monks to disturb the peace of the dunes, or the Rectory garden, in fact Nigel and Julie have felt a real sense of calm that had never been present in their home or garden before now. Ever since they had moved to the house a few years ago they had each felt, that something was not quite right but neither of them told the other of their disquiet, only since the burial of the bones had they each felt able to discuss it.

Every week now Nigel, when no one is about goes to the church and stands by the burials of the monks, women and children, he says a prayer and leaves a single flower on the grave of the five year old, child. A tear falls every time he does this, but he knows it will be a routine he will keep up until the day he dies. He feels responsible in part for those wicked murders so long ago, because a few years ago he took a DNA genealogy test, which found his family origins dwelled in Denmark, he might well be a descendant of the Viking that slew the little boy so many hundreds of years ago.

The Rev Rosemary Fitter has settled down to village life, occasionally having an evening no strings attached at the theatre in Reedsthorpe, with Col James-Fitzroy, encouraged by Dorothy who has put aside her personal needs or lusts for the sake of her friend, at least for the time being anyway. As a consequence, a happier Rosemary has emerged, and the village community have found themselves with an over indulgence of pastoral care, and no one has seen Rosemary tipsy for some time now.

Sophie and Geoffrey continue to enjoy a close friendship, and they both continue to support the local Priory Bird Watching Group, and Sophie occasionally gets Geoffrey to join her when she attends meetings of the Melton-Uppbury Historical Group.

The highlight of the year for the Priory Birders was when they spent the day at the Annual Bird Fair at Rutland Water in August; they met Chris Packham, and saw Bill Oddie. Sophie couldn't believe just how popular bird watching was; thousands of people went to it. Some even came as Bill Oddie lookalikes. Bill Taylor met up with a few old friends, and went on a short boat trip on the man made lake. The Priory Birders jointly decided whilst enjoying a meal in the cafeteria at the Bird Fair, to put the event on their annual calendar of events for the foreseeable future.

As Bill said to Felicity Oundle over coffee, 'Well I have to admit, Felicity that our past trips to the RSPB at Sandy don't hold a candle to this event, I'm afraid I'd got a bit set in my ways, and I am sorry I was a bit peeved at you, when you first suggested coming here.' Felicity smiled as Shelia Taylor winked at her across the table.

The Old Rectory
Church Lane
Melton –Uppbury
East Lincolnshire

Dear Reader

I hope you have enjoyed reading the latest occurrences that have happened in our village over the last year or so. For my wife Julie and I the recovery of the bones of the Anglo-Saxon monks and their families was quite traumatic. To think that we had both been pottering about in the garden over this last few years, whilst these poor souls have been buried just inches beneath the ground surface. Their end was indeed inhuman; such depraved treatment of fellow human beings is beyond my wife's and my comprehension. Yet when we watch the television news the world hasn't changed one iota. People are indeed cruel, yet occasionally we see a chink of light where someone or some community does something extraordinary, something kindly, benevolent something humane.

The invasion of the bird watching twitchers was upsetting to most villagers, but the main instigator of it Joseph Sinclair; turned out to be quite a decent chap, his generosity did much more than repair the damage done by his followers, he also gave our local nature reserve a decently surfaced car park, added to which the pub car park was also similarly given a much needed face lift. The local bird watching club, the Priory Birders may have lost their rare bird, but they ended up with five spanking new bird hides overlooking the fenlands, a great boost for their members, and indeed a great encouragement for people of all ages to engage in this popular pastime, but I for the time being at least, will stick to my archaeology. The traitor, who let the cat out of the bag about the gyrfalcon, was identified and he in the end helped put an ardent wicked egg collector out of business for a few years at least.

Jolene Appleyard's Riding School will soon be up and running, Zoe Weatherspoon has already had a few free lessons there, as if she hadn't enough hobbies already, archaeology, bird watching, and preparing an application for a University Archaeology course at Lincoln. It's strange to me how some young folk in their teens spend their time in bed till mid-morning, spending their nights out on the town, and others like Zoe take a hold of life and embrace it fully. When we did the dig in my garden, she was always there first, at the crack of dawn, and last to pack up her trowel.

Rosemary and James seem to be getting closer, which is nice to see, Julie thinks they'll make a perfect match despite the age difference and she should know.

Enid Barrheads beloved little Scottie dog Truffles has been ill for a week or two now, we all hope and pray he will be okay, Enid would be devastated if she lost him.

I hope you will in due course return to our village, quiet and sometimes mundane it might appear to be, but not always so.

Yours Sincerely,

Nigel Clutterbuck

Characters

Fred Allsop (61): Owner of Melton Uppbury Boat Yard. Has a house at the boatyard.

Mrs Bottomly (58): Chair off the Parochial Church Council and member of Parish Council. Lives in the bungalows.

Enid Barrhead (70): Retired village Librarian lives in Melton Uppbury with her dog Truffles, in one of the seafront cottages.

Nigel Clutterbuck (69): Dr (Retired GP) Amateur Archaeologist. Lives with his wife at the Old Rectory.

Julie Clutterbuck (58): Wife of Dr Clutterbuck former Physiotherapist.

Gerald Parker (55): Owner of the General Store in nearby Reedsthorpe. Chairman, of the Melton-Uppbury Parish Council. Lives in bungalows.

Alf Prichard (31): Unemployed. (Metal Detectorist) lives on the council estate.

Silas Pestell (68): Owner of Pestell Antiques Emporium in Melton Uppbury. Lives above shop.

Harry Weatherspoon (41): Co-owner of the Melton-Uppbury Village Post Office/Store. Lives in shop flat.

Kate Weather spoon (40): Co-owner of the Melton-Uppbury Village Post Office/Store. Lives in shop flat.

Colonel James Smith-Fitzroy (55): (Ret Cold Stream Guards) Publican owner of the Crows Roost Inn in Melton-Uppbury. Lives in flat above the pub.

Helen (32): Barmaid at the Crows Roost Inn; lives in Reedsthorpe.

Jack Wilkinson (72): Honorary Secretary of the Friends of Reedsthorpe Museum. Lives in Reedsthorpe.

Rosemary Fitter (36): Rector of St Guthlac's Parish Church, temporarily homeless.

Jake Purdy (64): Gypsy with 5 dogs. lives on Council Estate.

Mrs Slater (75): Owner of the village caravan site widow of local Farmer, lives in a cottage at the top end of the village.

Mrs Alderton (81): Elderly widow formerly a close friend of the late vicar. Lives on the council estate.

James Sudbury: late Vicar of St Guthlac's.

Sophie Weatherspoon (16): Daughter of Harry and Kate. Weatherspoon, lives above parents shop.

Roland Barrhead: Late husband of Enid former Bank Manager.

Patsy Clyde 51): Owner of the Beach Café; lives at nearby Claythorpe on Sea.

Cyril Merrick (62): Owns and lives at Home Farm.

John Merrick (66): Owns Merrick's Stables. Lives in mobile home at the stables.

Dorothy Burton (25): Theology Student at the Lincoln Theological College. Living in Lincoln.

Mr Higgins (?): Chair of St George's Church Parochial Church Council, in Reedsthorpe.

Zoe Hartington nee Lake (38): Archaeologist Curator of Antiquities Lincoln Museum. Lives in Lincoln.

Mike Hartington (40): Archaeologist, husband of Zoe, lives in Lincoln.

Len (59): St Guthlac's Church part time Sexton and handyman, lives on the council estate.

Sidney Harding (44): Accountant based in Reedsthorpe. Lives in Reedsthorpe.

Rufford Family: Reedsthorpe Garden Centre.

John White (52): Village Newcomer lives in bungalows.

Bill and Shelia Taylor (70s): Organiser's of the Priory Birders. Live in the bungalows.

Felicity Oundle (33): Nurse from Reedsthorpe member of the Priory Birders club.

Geoffrey Thompson (20): Newcomer and Young Bird Watcher. Lives on the council estate with his parents.

Nurses: Martha, Margaret, Emma and Janet from Reedsthorpe Hospital.

Tony (18): Nurse Martha's son.

Joseph Sinclair: (58) Sinclair Electronics. Twitchers leader.

Andrew Appleyard (60): Reedsthorpe Car Dealer.

Mavis Appleyard (54): Wife of Andrew Appleyard.

Jolene Appleyard (25): Daughter of Andrew and Mavis.

Michael (62): The Angry Tall Thin Man, Egg Collector.

John (22): Museum Archaeology Volunteer.

Lewis (18): Museum Archaeology Volunteer.

Printed in Poland
by Amazon Fulfillment
Poland Sp. z o.o., Wrocław